JOHNSON COUNTY PUBLIC LIBRARY

3 2938 00055 6616

S0-BEA-428

11-87 J FIC YOL
Yolen, Jane.
A sending of dragons.

WHITE RIVER LIBRARY
FRANKLIN-JOHNSON COUNTY
PUBLIC LIBRARY
401 South State Street
Franklin, IN 46131-2545

1 3/05

61 04
③

WITHDRAWN

① 4/9/05

15364966   SAW

a sending of dragons

Also by Jane Yolen

The Pit Dragon Trilogy
DRAGON'S BLOOD
HEART'S BLOOD
A SENDING OF DRAGONS

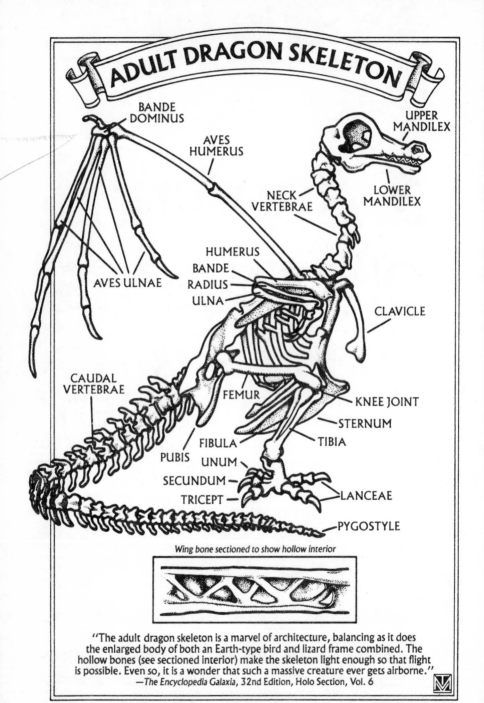

ADULT DRAGON SKELETON

BANDE DOMINUS

AVES HUMERUS

UPPER MANDILEX

LOWER MANDILEX

NECK VERTEBRAE

HUMERUS

BANDE

RADIUS

ULNA

AVES ULNAE

CLAVICLE

CAUDAL VERTEBRAE

FEMUR

KNEE JOINT

STERNUM

TIBIA

FIBULA

PUBIS

UNUM

SECUNDUM

TRICEPT

LANCEAE

PYGOSTYLE

Wing bone sectioned to show hollow interior

"The adult dragon skeleton is a marvel of architecture, balancing as it does the enlarged body of both an Earth-type bird and lizard frame combined. The hollow bones (see sectioned interior) make the skeleton light enough so that flight is possible. Even so, it is a wonder that such a massive creature ever gets airborne."
—*The Encyclopedia Galaxia*, 32nd Edition, Holo Section, Vol. 6

a sending of dragons

pit dragons: book 3

jane yolen

delacorte press / new york

WHITE RIVER LIBRARY
Franklin-Johnson County System
Franklin, IN 46131

Published by
Delacorte Press
1 Dag Hammarskjold Plaza
New York, New York   10017

Drawings by Thomas McKeveny

Text copyright © 1987 by Jane Yolen
Map & Drawing copyright © 1987 by Thomas McKeveny

All rights reserved. No part of this book may be reproduced or transmitted in any form or by any means, electronic or mechanical, including photocopying, recording or by any information storage and retrieval system, without the written permission of the Publisher, except where permitted by law.

MANUFACTURED IN THE UNITED STATES OF AMERICA

FIRST PRINTING

Library of Congress Cataloging-in-Publication Data
Yolen, Jane.
   A sending of dragons.
   Summary: Falsely accused of sabotage, Jakkin and Akki
are sent out to certain death in the wilderness of the
planet Austar IV but, through the heroic sacrifice of
Jakkin's dragon and the help of her offspring, manage
not only to survive but gain unusual powers and insights.
   [1. Dragons—Fiction.   2. Fantasy]   I. Title.
PZ7.Y78Sd   1987   [Fic]   87-6689
ISBN 0-385-29587-1

y
Copy 1

For Jonathan Grenzke,
dragon master,
shatterer of a thousand shields,
who lives right down the road

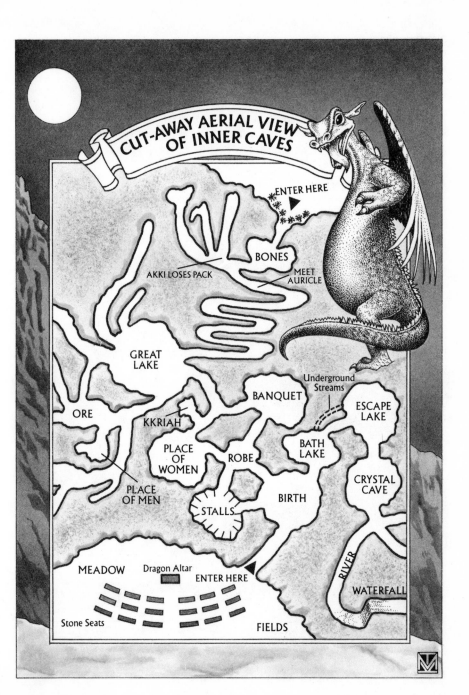

Austar IV is the fourth planet of a seven-planet rim system in the Erato Galaxy. Once a penal colony, marked KK29 on the convict map system, it is a semiarid, metal-poor world with two moons.

Austar is covered by vast deserts, some of which are cut through by small and irregularly surfacing hot springs, several small sections of fenlands, and zones of what were long thought to be impenetrable mountains charted only by the twice-yearly flyovers by Federation ships. There are only five major rivers: the Narrakka, the Rokk, the Brokk-bend, the Kkar, and the Left Forkk.

Few plants grow in the deserts—some fruit cacti and sparse long-trunk palm trees known as spikka. The most populous plants on Austar are two wild-flowering bushes called burnwort and blisterweed. (See color section.) The mountain vegetation, only recently studied, is varied and includes many edible fungi, berry bushes, and a low oily grass called Skkagg, which, when boiled, produces a thin broth high in vitamin content.

There is a variety of insect and pseudolizard life, the latter ranging from small rock-runners to elephant-sized dragons. (See holo sections, Vol. 6.) Unlike Earth *reptilia*, the Austarian dragon lizards are warm-blooded, with pneumaticized bones for reduction of weight and a keeled sternum where the flight muscles are attached. They have membranous wings with jointed ribs that fold back along the animals' bodies when the dragons are earthbound. Stretched to the fullest, an adult dragon's wings are twice its body size. The "feathers" are actually light scales which adjust to wind pressure. From claw to shoulder, some specimens of Austarian dragons have been measured at thirteen feet. There is increasing evidence of a level 4+ intelligence and a color-coded telepathic mode of communication in the Austarian dragons. These great beasts were almost extinct when the planet was first settled by convicts (or KKs as they called themselves) and guards from Earth in 2303. But several generations later the Austarians domesticated the few remaining dragons, selectively breeding them for meat and leather and the gaming arenas—or, as they were known from earliest times, the Pits.

The dragon Pits of Austar IV were more than just the main entertainment for early KKs. Over the years the Pits have become central to the Austarian economy. Betting syndicates developed and Federation starship crews on long rim-world voyages began to frequent the planet on gambling forays.

Because such gambling violated current Galaxian law, illegal offworld gamesters were expelled in 2485 from Austar IV and imprisoned on penal planet KK47, Sedna, a mining colony where most of the surface is ice-covered. Under pressure from the Federation, the Austarians then drafted a Protectorate constitution spelling out the Federation's administrative role in the economy of the planet, including regulation of the gambling of offworlders and the payment of taxes (which Austarians call tithing) on gambling moneys in exchange for starship landing bases. A fluid caste system of masters and bond slaves—the remnants of the convict-guard hierarchy—was established by law, with a bond price set as an entrance fee into the master class. Established at the same time was a Senate, the members of which come exclusively from the master class. The Senate performs both the executive and legislative functions of the Austarian government and, for the most part, represents all the interests of the Federation in Austarian matters. As with all Protectorate planets, offworlders are subject to the local laws and liable to the same punishments for breaking them.

The Rokk, which was a fortress inhabited by the original ruling guards and their families when Austar IV was a penal planet, is now the capital city and the starship landfall.

In the mid 2500s disgruntled bonders, angry with their low place in Austarian society and the inequities visited upon their class, began to foment a revolution, which broke into violent confrontations. The worst of these was the bombing of Rokk Major, the greatest gaming Pit on the planet. Thirty-seven people were killed outright, twenty-three died of their wounds in the months that followed. Hundreds of other people, both Austarians and offworlders, were seriously injured. It was the beginning of several years of internal conflict which, according to Federation rules, led to the closing of Austar to Federation ships by means of a fifty-year embargo. This embargo was imposed in 2543 and kept all official ships from landing, which meant Austar IV was without sanctioned metal and technical assistance for that period of time. Occasional pirate ships slipped through the embargo lines, and intercepted coded transmissions from the ships indicate that there is more than the simple expected master-bonder power struggle being waged on the planet. Frequent references to Dragon Masters and Dragonmen remain unclear. The complete story of Austar IV will probably not be known until the Federation embargo is lifted and the Austarians speak for themselves.

—Excerpt from *The Encyclopedia Galaxia,*
32nd Edition, Vol. 1: Aaabarker—Austar

the
hatchlings

1

Night was approaching. The umber moon led its pale, shadowy brother across the multicolored sky. In front of the moons flew five dragons.

The first was the largest, its great wings dipping and rising in an alien semaphore. Directly behind it were three smaller fliers, wheeling and circling, tagging one another's tails. In the rear, along a lower trajectory, sailed a middle-sized and plumper version of the front dragon. More like a broom than a rudder, its tail seemed to sweep across the faces of the moons.

Jakkin watched them, his right hand shading his eyes. Squatting on his haunches in front of a mountain cave, he was nearly naked except for a pair of white pants cut off at mid-thigh, a concession to modesty rather than a help against the oncoming cold night. He was burned brown everywhere but for three small pits on his back, which remained white despite their long exposure to the sun. Slowly Jakkin stood, running grimy fingers through his shoulder-length hair, and shouted up at the hatchlings.

"Fine flying, my friends!" The sound of his voice caromed off the mountains, but the dragons gave no sign they heard him. So he sent the same message with his mind in the rainbow-colored patterns with which he and the dragons communicated. *Fine flying.* The picture he sent was of gray-green wings with air rushing through the leathery feathers, tickling each link. *Fine flying.* He was sure his sending could reach them, but none of the dragons responded.

Jakkin stood for a moment longer watching the flight. He took pleasure in the hatchlings' airborne majesty. Even though they were still awkward on the ground, a sure sign of their youth, against the sky they were already an awesome sight.

Jakkin took pleasure as well in the colors surrounding the dragons. Though he'd lived months now in the Austarian wilds, he hadn't tired of the evening's purples and reds, roses and blues, the ever-changing display that signaled the approaching night. Before he'd been *changed*, as he called it, he'd hardly seen the colors. Evenings had been a time of darkening and the threat of Dark After, the bone-chilling, killing cold. Every Austarian knew better than to be caught outside in it. But now both Dark After and dawn were his, thanks to the *change*.

"Ours!" The message invaded his mind in a ribbon of laughter. *"Dark After and dawn are ours now."* The sending came a minute before its sender appeared around a bend in the mountain path.

Jakkin waited patiently. He knew Akki would be close behind, for the sending had been strong and Akki couldn't broadcast over a long range.

She came around the bend with cheeks rosy from running. Her dark braid was tied back with a fresh-plaited vine. Jakkin preferred it when she let her hair loose, like a black curtain around her face, but he'd never been able to tell her so. She carried a reed basket full of food for their dinner. Speaking aloud in a tumble of words, she ran toward him. "Jakkin, I've found a whole new meadow and . . ."

He went up the path to meet her and dipped his hand into the basket. Before she could pull it away, he'd snagged a single pink chikkberry. Then she grabbed the basket, putting it safely behind her.

"All right, worm waste, what have you been doing while I found our dinner?" Her voice was stern, but she couldn't hide the undercurrent of thought, which was sunny, golden, laughing.

"I've been working too," he said, careful to speak out loud. Akki still preferred speech to sendings when they were face-to-face. She said speech had a precision to it that the sendings lacked, that it was clearer for everything but emotions. She was quite fierce about it. It was an argument Jakkin didn't want to venture into again. "I've some interesting things—"

Before he could finish, five small streamlike sendings teased into his head, a confusion of colored images, half-visualized.

"Jakkin . . . the sky . . . see the moons . . . wind and wings, ah . . . see, see . . ."

Jakkin spun away from Akki and cried out to the dragons, a wild, high yodeling that bounced off the mountains. With it he sent another kind of call, a web of fine traceries with the names of the hatchlings woven within: Sssargon, Sssasha, and the triplets Tri-sss, Tri-ssskkette, and Tri-sssha.

"Fewmets!" Akki complained. "That's too loud. Here I am, standing right next to you, and you've fried me." She set the basket down on an outjut of rock and rubbed her temples vigorously.

Jakkin knew she meant the mind sending had been too loud and had left her with a head full of brilliant hot lights. He'd had weeks of similar headaches when Akki first began sending, until they'd both learned to adjust. "Sorry," he whispered, taking a turn at rubbing her head over the ears, where the hot ache lingered. "Sometimes I forget. It takes so much more to make a dragon complain and their brains never get fried."

"Brains? What brains? Everyone knows dragons haven't any brains. Just muscle and bone and . . ."

". . . and claws and teeth," Jakkin finished for her, then broke into the chorus of the Pit song she'd referred to:

> *"Muscle and bone*
> *And claws and teeth,*
> *Fire above and*
> *Fewmets beneath."*

Akki laughed, just as he'd hoped, for laughter usually bled away the pain of a close sending. She came over and hugged him, and just as her arms went around, the true Austarian darkness closed in.

"You've got some power," Jakkin said. "One hug—and the lights go out!"

"Wait until you see what I do at dawn," she replied, giving a mock shiver.

To other humans the Austarian night was black and pitiless and the false dawn, Dark After, mortally cold. Even an hour outside during that time of bone-chill meant certain death. But Jakkin and Akki were different now, different from all their friends at the dragon nursery, different from the trainers and bondboys at the Pits, different from the men who slaughtered dragons in the Stews or the girls who filled their bondbags with money made in the baggeries. They were different from anyone in the history of Austar IV because they had been *changed.*

Jakkin's thoughts turned as dark as the oncoming night, remembering just how they'd been *changed*. Chased into the mountains by wardens for the bombing of Rokk Major, which they had not really committed, they'd watched helplessly as Jakkin's great red dragon, Heart's Blood, had taken shots meant for them, dying as she tried to protect them. And then, left by the wardens to the oncoming cold, they had sheltered in Heart's Blood's body, in the very chamber where she'd recently carried eggs, and had emerged, somehow able to stand the cold and share their thoughts. He shut the memory down. Even months later it was too painful. Pulling himself away from the past, he realized he was still in the circle of Akki's arms. Her face showed deep concern, and he realized she'd been listening in on his thoughts. But when she spoke it was on a different subject altogether, and for that he was profoundly grateful.

"Come see what I found today," she said quietly, pulling him over to the basket. "Not just berries, but a new kind of mushroom. They were near a tiny cave on the south face of the Crag." Akki insisted on naming things because—she said—that made them more real. Mountains, meadows, vegetations, caves —they all bore her imprint. "We can test them out, first uncooked and later in with some Boil soup. I nibbled a bit about an hour ago and haven't had any bad effects, so they're safe. You'll like these, Jakkin. They may look like Cave Apples, but I found them under a small tree. I call them Meadow Apples."

Jakkin made a face. He wasn't fond of mushrooms, and Cave Apples were the worst.

"They're sweeter than you think."

Anything, Jakkin thought, would be sweeter than the round, reddish Cave Apples with their musty, dusty taste, but he worried about Akki nibbling on unknown mushrooms. What if they were poisonous and she was all alone on the mountainside?

Both thoughts communicated immediately to Akki and she swatted him playfully on the chest. "Cave Apples are good for you, Jakkin. High in protein. I learned that from Dr. Henkky when I studied with her in The Rokk. Besides, if I didn't test these out, we might miss something good. Don't be such a worrier. I checked with Sssasha first and she said dragons love them."

"Dragons love burnwort too," muttered Jakkin. "And I'd sure hate to try and eat it, even if it *could* help me breathe fire."

"Listen, Jakkin Stewart, it's either mushrooms—or back to eating dragon stew. We have to have protein to live." Her eyes narrowed.

Jakkin shrugged as if to say he didn't care, but his thoughts broadcast his true feelings to her. They both knew they'd never eat meat again. Now that they could talk mind-to-mind with Heart's Blood's hatchlings and even pass shadowy thoughts with some of the lesser creatures like lizards and rock-runners, eating meat was unthinkable.

"If Meadow Apples are better than Cave Apples," Jakkin said aloud, "I'm sure I'll love them. Besides, I'm starving!"

"You and the dragons," Akki said. "That's all they ever think about too. Food, food, food. But the question is—do you deserve my hard-found food?"

"I've been working too," Jakkin said. "I'm trying to make some better bowls to put your hard-found food in. I discovered a new clay bank down the cliff and across Lower Meadows. You know . . ."

Akki did know, because he never went near Upper Meadows, where Heart's Blood's bones still lay, picked clean by the mountain scavengers. He went down toward the Lower Meadows and she scouted farther up. He could read her thoughts as clearly as she could read his.

He continued out loud, ". . . there's a kind of swamp there, the start of a small river, pooling down from the mountain streams. The mountain is covered with them. But I'd never seen this particular one before because it's hard to get to. This clay is the best I've found so far and I managed a whole sling of it. Maybe in a night or two we can build a fire and try to bake the pots I've made."

They both knew bake fires could be set only at night, later than any humans would be out. *Just in case.* Only at night did they feel totally safe from the people who had chased them into the mountains: the murderous wardens who had followed them from the bombed-out Pit to the dragon nursery and from there up into the mountains, and the even more murderous rebels who, in the name of "freedom," had fooled them into destroying the great Rokk Major Dragon Pit. All those people thought them dead, from hunger or cold or from being crushed when Heart's Blood fell. It was best they continue to believe it. So the first rule of mountain life, they'd agreed, was *Take no chances.*

"Never mind that, Jakkin," Akki said. "Don't think about it. The past is the past. Let it go. Let's enjoy what we have now. Show me your new pots, and then we can eat."

They walked into the cave, one of three they'd claimed as their own. Though Jakkin still thought of them as numbers— one, two, and three—Akki had named them. The cave in the Lower Meadows was Golden's Cave, named after their friend who had fled with them and had most certainly died at the wardens' hands. Golden's Cave had caches of berries for flavoring and for drinks. Akki had strung dried flowers on vines that made a rustly curtain between the main cave and the smaller sleeping quarters, which they kept private from the dragons. Higher on the mountain, but not as high as the Upper Meadows, was Likkarn's Lookout. It was as rough and uncompromising a place as the man it was named after, Jakkin's old trainer and enemy Likkarn. But Likkarn had proved a surprising ally in the end, and so had the lookout cave, serving them several times in the early days of their exile when they'd spotted bands of searchers down in the valley. But the middle cave, which Akki called the New Nursery, was the one they really considered their home.

What had first drawn them to it had been its size. It had a great hollow vaulted room with a succession of smaller caves behind. There were wonderful ledges at different levels along the walls on which Jakkin's unfired clay bowls and canisters sat. Ungainly and thick the clay pots certainly were, but Jakkin's skills were improving with each try, and the bowls, if not pretty, were functional, holding stashes of chikkberries, dried mushrooms like the cave apples Jakkin so disliked, and edible grasses. So far his own favorite bit of work was a large-bellied jar containing Boil. It was the one piece he had successfully fired and it was hard and did not leak.

The floor of the cave was covered with dried grasses that lent a sharp sweet odor to the air. There was a mattress of the same grass, which they changed every few days. The bed lay in one of the small inner chambers where, beneath a natural chimney, they could look up at night and see the stars.

"There!" Jakkin said, pointing to the shelf that held his latest still-damp work. "This clay was a lot easier to work."

There were five new pots, one large bowl, and two slightly lopsided drinking cups.

"What do you think?"

"Oh, Jakkin, they're the best yet. When they're dry we *must* try them in the fire. What do *you* think?"

"I think . . ." And then he laughed, shaping a picture of an enormous cave apple in his mind. The mushroom had an enormous bite-sized chunk out of it.

Akki laughed. "If you are hungry enough to think about eating *that*," she said, "we'd better start the dinner right away!"

"We come. Have hunger too." The sendings from the three smallest dragons broke into Jakkin's head. Their signature colors were shades of pink and rose.

"We wait. We ride your shoulder. Our eyes are yours." That came from the largest two of Heart's Blood's hatchlings. They were already able to travel miles with neither hunger nor fatigue, and their sendings had matured to a deeper red. Sssargon and Sssasha, the names they had given themselves with the characteristic dragon hiss at the beginning, spent most of the daylight hours catching currents of air that carried them over the jagged mountain peaks. They were, as they called themselves, Jakkin's and Akki's eyes, a mobile warning signal. But they were not needed for scouting at night because there was nothing Jakkin and Akki feared once the true dark set in.

"Come home. Come home." Jakkin's sending was a green vine of thought.

"Yes, come home." Akki's sending, much weaker than Jakkin's, was a twining of blue strands around his brighter green. Blue and green, the braiding of the cooler human colors.

"Come home," called the blue once again. *"Come home. I have much food. And I have a new song for you."* The sending was soothing and inviting at the same time. The young dragons

loved songs, loved the thrumming, humming sounds, especially if the songs concerned great flying worms. Baby dragons, Akki's thought passed along to Jakkin, thought mostly about two things —themselves and what they wanted to eat.

2

"They'll be here soon," Akki said in the sensible tone she often used when talking about the hatchlings. "So we'd better eat. You know how much attention they demand once they're down—rubbing and coaxing and ear scratching."

"Nursery dragons are worse," reminded Jakkin. "They can't do anything for themselves. Except eat. At least these are finding grazing on their own. And they groom themselves. And . . ."

"They're still babies, though."

"Some babies!" Jakkin laughed and held his hand above Akki's head. Sssargon's broad back already came that high, and with his long ridged neck and enormous head, he was twice Jakkin's height and still growing.

"Big babies!" Akki amended.

They laughed aloud together and then walked to the pathway, where they sat down on the flat rocks flanking the cave mouth. Akki shared out the bits of mushroom and then the berries. She had found three kinds: tart chikkberries, black and juicy warden's heart, and the dry, pebbly wormseye. They washed the meal down with a cup of Boil, the thin soup made from cooking the greasy brown skkagg grass of the high meadow. Boil was only drinkable cold—and then just barely. Jakkin made a face.

"I still miss a cup of hot takk with my dinner," he said. He wiped away a purple smear from his mouth, a trace of warden's heart, and slowly looked up at the sky. A dark smudge in the west resolved itself into a dragon form. As it came closer, Jakkin stood.

"Sssargon come." Sssargon always announced himself, keeping up a running commentary on his actions. *"Sssargon lands."*

His wings stirred the dust at the cave mouth, and for a moment obscured his landing, but Jakkin knew it was a perfect touchdown. For such a large and clumsy-looking beast, Sssargon was often quite dainty.

"Sssargon folds wings." The great pinions swept back against his sides, the scaly feathers fluttering for just a moment before quieting. Sssargon squatted, then let his large ribbed tongue flick in and out between his jaws. *"Sssargon hungers."*

Jakkin went back into the cave and came out with a handful of wild burnwort, just enough to take the edge off Sssargon's hunger and to quiet his pronouncements. Though Heart's Blood's hatchlings had begun to graze on their own in the various high meadows full of wort and weed, they hated giving up their ritual of sharing. Jakkin had to admit that he also hated to think about giving it up. He smiled tenderly at the dragon.

"Big babies," Akki whispered.

Jakkin ignored her and focused on Sssargon. "Here, big fellow," he said aloud, adding a quick green-tinged visualization of the wort.

Sssargon's rough tongue snagged the plant from Jakkin's hand and his answer was the crisp snip-snap of wort being crunched between his teeth.

Sssasha landed just as Sssargon began to eat, with neither fanfare nor commentary. She stepped over his outstretched tail but folded her wings a second too soon, which made her cant to one side. She had to flip her outside wing open again in order to right herself.

The red flicker of amusement that Sssargon sent through all their minds made Jakkin sputter. Akki broke into a cascade of giggles, but Sssasha was too even-tempered to mind. She was as sunny as the splash of gold across her nose, a slash of color that— along with her even disposition and placid ways—would have made her unfit either to fight in the Pits as her mother, Heart's Blood, had or to be considered for spaying and dwarfing as a *beauty*, a house pet. Jakkin realized, with a kind of dawning horror, that Sssasha would have been one of the early culls in the nurseries, where hatchlings were bred for only one of three destinies. The bonders said, *Pit, pet, or stew.* Jakkin swallowed hastily at the thought of Sssasha in one of the Stews, a green-suited steward standing over her, placing a stinger to her ear, a knife at her throat. He bit his lip, all laughter gone.

"What pain?" Sssasha's question poked into his mind.

"No pain," Jakkin said aloud, but his mind transferred a different thought.

"Yes, pain," insisted Sssasha.

"Old pain. Gone." Jakkin made his mind a careful blank. It was hard work, and he could feel himself starting to perspire.

"Good," said Sssasha.

"Yesssssss, good," Sssargon interrupted suddenly, exploding red bomb bursts in Jakkin's head. *"Sssargon have great hunger."*

Akki, who had been following this silent exchange thoughtfully, soothed them all with a picture of a cool blue rain, holding

it in mind long enough for Jakkin to go back into the cave for
two more large handfuls of wort.

Once in the cave, Jakkin was able to let his guard down for a
minute, though he reminded himself that even in the cool darkness of the cave, behind walls of stone, he could not be private.
His mind was an open invitation to Akki or any dragon who
wanted to enter it. Only with the most careful and arduous
concentration could he guard its entrance. He had to visualize a
wall built up plank by plank or a heavy drapery drawn across it
inch by inch. And usually by the time he had carefully constructed these images, the traitor thoughts had already slipped
out. He wondered how dragons kept secrets or even if they had
secrets to keep. Everything he thought or felt was now open and
public.

"Open to me anyway," Akki said as Jakkin emerged from the
cave.

He realized with sudden chagrin that she had been listening
to his self-pitying thoughts. The more powerful the emotion, the
farther it seemed to broadcast. Akki, listening quietly, had sent
nothing in return. Flushing with embarrassment, Jakkin looked
down at the ground, trying to think of a way to phrase what he
had to say out loud. He knew he could control words, because he
didn't actually have to *say* anything until he was ready. At last he
spoke. "Sometimes," he began reluctantly, "sometimes a man
needs to be alone." He held out the wort to Sssargon and concentrated totally on that.

"Sometimes," Akki said to his back, "sometimes a *woman*
needs to be alone too."

He turned his head to apologize. Words, it seemed, could be
slippery too. But Akki wasn't looking at him. She had her hands
up to her eyes, as if shading them from the too-colorful dark.

"Jakkin, this is a strange gift we've been given, being able to sneak into one another's minds. But . . ."

"But at least we're together," Jakkin said, suddenly afraid of what else Akki might say, suddenly afraid that the words, more than any thoughts, might hurt terribly.

"We may be together more than we ever meant to be," Akki said. But even as she said it she touched his hand.

He concentrated on that touch and let the rest of it go, making his mind a blank slate like the evening sky. At last little spear points of violet blue pushed across that blank and Jakkin realized Akki was worried.

"Where are the triplets?" she asked. "They should have been here by now. And that's a worry I don't mind sharing."

"Sssargon not worry. You not worry." Munching contentedly on the last few straws of wort, the dragon gave off waves of mindless serenity. His mood changed only when he noticed that he had finished what was in his mouth, at which point he stretched his neck out to its greatest length and stole a few bites from his sister.

"That's very reassuring, Sssargon," Akki sent.

Jakkin could only guess at the sarcasm behind her thought. There was no color translation for it.

Sssasha let Sssargon take the last of her wort and rose clumsily. She clambered toward Jakkin to see if she could nose out some more food. Bumping against his shoulder, she nearly knocked him to the ground.

"Fewmets!" he cried out. "I may be able to see and hear like a dragon now, but I still can't fly, Sssasha. If you knock me off the mountain, I'll land *splat!*" He tried to send the sound of it with his mind.

"?????"

"Splat!" Jakkin said, then shouted, "SPLAT!"

Akki cupped her hand and slapped it against the dragon's haunch. It made a strange sound.

Sssasha blinked, then sent a barrage of red bubbles into Jakkin's mind. Each one burst with a noise that sounded remarkably like *splat!*

"Exactly," Jakkin said aloud. "And if you think that sounds funny, you should see how funny I'd look *splat*tered all over the landscape." His laugh was a short barking sound.

But the joke was untranslatable to the dragon and all she received was an unfocused color picture of Jakkin's mood: a net of wistfulness, a slash of anger, and a wisp of lingering self-pity. She turned her head away and gazed out across the mountains that edged into the valley below. If she was amused or worried or upset, no one could tell from her rosy sending and her casual stance.

"Dragons!" Jakkin muttered to himself. Even with his dragon sight he could not pierce the darkness to see what drew her gaze, so he settled down next to her on his haunches, ran his hands through his hair, and waited.

It was five minutes before the triplets began sounding in his mind.

3

The high-pitched twittering chatter of the three hatchlings began to reach them. The sounds the trio made were unlike any of the full-throated roars Jakkin had ever heard from dragons in the fighting Pits. It was as if the three had invented a language all their own, which they occasionally slowed down so that listeners could make some sense of it. Their sendings, too, sputtered with color, which sometimes formed into readable pictures but as often remained unclear.

Moments later they sailed into view, wingtips apart. They flew in formation, their favorite trick. Inseparable, they might as well have emerged from the same egg, though in fact the eggs had been in totally different parts of the clutch. Still, they looked alike, a rough brown color undistinguished by any markings, and their sending signatures were remarkably alike too. In honor of their being such close triplets, Akki had named them Tri-sss, Tri-sssha, and Tri-ssskkette. They had accepted those names without a murmur of dissent. But all together they were addressed as Tri, and all three answered to the one name. If they had any others they preferred, it was a secret they shared with no one.

Landing together on the upper edge of the ledge, they waddled in step single file down the trail.

"Men coming, men coming, men coming," they sent, one right after another.

"It's dark and will soon be Dark After," said Jakkin.

Rubbing Tri-sssha behind the ears, Akki added, "And you know men can't live in the cold."

"You men. You men. You here." Tri-sssha, earflaps vibrating from the special attention, managed a different phrase.

"Yes, but we're different," Akki explained patiently.

"Men coming. Men coming. Men coming," insisted the little dragons, ignoring both Akki's explanation and the food that Jakkin held out to them.

The minute they turned their heads aside to look up at the darkened sky, Sssargon stretched his long neck, moving his head within inches of Jakkin's. His tongue snaked out and deftly removed the wort from Jakkin's hand. Jakkin slapped at the dragon's nose an instant too late.

And then Jakkin heard a strange mechanical chuffing, the sound of a copter in the distance. It was a noise rarely heard outside The Rokk, the main city, where such devices belonged only to Federation officials or starship crews. No one on Austar was allowed them.

"Akki!" Jakkin cried out loud.

"I hear it," she said, fear touching her eyes before her mind sent its notice.

"Men coming, men coming, men coming," the trio of hatchlings sent out again in arrow points, and the larger two dragons, from their perch on the mountain, picked up the chorus. They'd been linked to their dragon mother, Heart's Blood, when she

had died under the guns of men, and they harbored a great distrust of humans, except for Jakkin and Akki.

Sssargon lifted his head and swiveled it about like a periscope. A bright light in his black eyes flickered for a moment. Then he addressed Jakkin formally, mind-to-mind. *"Sssargon flies."*

"No, Sssargon!" Akki cried, stretching her hand out to him.

"No!" commanded Jakkin, deliberately using the tone of voice he normally reserved for the training sessions in which he taught the dragons the fighting moves of the great Pits.

But this time Sssargon, usually the most eager at training, ignored Jakkin's demand and stretched his wings. Pumping them twice, he leaped off the cliffside, immediately catching an updraft, and sailed away.

"He's only a baby," whispered Akki. "A baby."

Jakkin strained to watch the dragon as he disappeared in the night sky. "Are we so much older?"

"I feel about a hundred years older," said Akki in a quiet, tired voice. She herded the hatchlings into the cave before her and looked over her shoulder at Jakkin. "A hundred hundred years."

He followed them in.

The cave was large, but the four growing hatchlings crowded things considerably and Sssasha, as usual, managed to bump into a shelf, knocking off two of the new bowls.

"Splat?"

Even Jakkin had to laugh at that. He sat down with his back to the cave wall and hoped the cool rock would keep him from sweating too much. Four dragons, even small ones, were like furnaces in the closed-in cave. He could feel the temperature beginning to rise.

Akki sat across from him with Tri-sssha's head in her lap. Her fingers caressed the dragon's earflaps, scratching all around.

Humming an old Pit ballad about a hen fighter who was matched against one of her own hatchlings, Akki was totally caught up in the sad, haunting melody. So was Tri-sssha. Jakkin could feel the dragon begin to thrum, her initial fears of the men in copters subsumed by the deep sounding of her own body. Tri-sss and Tri-ssskkette joined her, and soon the cave vibrated with it. When Sssasha finally lent her own deeper thrums to the lot, it was overpowering. Jakkin's head buzzed with the hum and the heat, and he felt it as a great pressure on his temples and chest.

"Stop it!" he cried out angrily, standing up and bumping his forehead on a jutting rock. The pain communicated in a way his anger had not.

Akki lifted her hands as if warding off a blow. The thrumming stopped.

"We have to think," Jakkin warned. "We have to think and watch and listen. Pay attention."

As he spoke an image formed in his mind, a sending from Sssargon. The helicopter was making a series of quick spiraling passes over the mountains. Sssargon drifted along lazily, looking like any wild dragon out for a late evening fly. He buzzed the helicopter once, then banked away as if satisfied that the metal bird was not a threat. Jakkin saw the copter through Sssargon's eyes: a heavy, mindless object in the middle of wind eddies, communicating great heat and nothing else. It had no feathers and no smell and seemed, in Sssargon's view, pilotless.

"The men inside," Jakkin sent to the dragon, trying to make his images clear. Landscape, emotion, things of the senses passed so easily through a sending, but other things . . . *"Look at the men inside, Sssargon. What do they wear? What do they look like?"* If Sssargon could send a description, they would know

who the men were—Federation rocket pilots or wardens or rebels. *"Look at the men."*

But the questions didn't seem to interest the dragon and neither did the men in the copter. He sent only a vague impression of a human at the throttle, and then, having tired of this latest game, banked to the right and returned to the ledge. They caught his sending announcing a perfect backwinged landing. *"Sssargon lands."* A slight thumping outside the cave as his heavy hind legs touched down confirmed this.

"Sssargon home. Sssargon home. Sssargon home." The three jubilant sendings heralded him.

"Sssargon home. Sssargon hungers. Scratch Sssargon."

"Hush!" Akki's voice overrode the sending. "And stay put. We're already too crowded in here." The hushing was really for Jakkin's benefit, for Sssargon had made no outward sounds. Like his mother before him, and like Sssasha, Sssargon was mute. Only those who could tune in on a dragon's sending could hear him. But his sendings were always louder than necessary, like a young boy clamoring for attention. "Hush," Akki repeated, her tone still commanding. But her sending to the dragon was far gentler.

Sssargon swept his wings back and lay down at the cave entrance, looking for all the world like a dozing dragon guarding his cache.

The copter flew by once more and, apparently satisfied, climbed the updraft and was gone.

4

The whir of the copter had faded long minutes past but still they sat in the cave, waiting. Sssargon hulked in the entrance.

At last Akki sighed. "We can go out now," she said, but she said it in a whisper. Then she laughed. "What an idiot I am. What idiots *we* are. They couldn't hear us with all that noise anyway."

Jakkin stood and started toward the cave entrance, wiping the sweat from his forehead as he went. The others followed after.

Sssargon refused to move.

"Sssargon stays. Sssargon's neck needs scratching. Sssargon hungers. Sssargon wants—"

"Sssargon shuts up!" Jakkin hissed at him, and pushed at the dragon's nose while simultaneously sending large blue daggers into the worm's mind. The dragon rose reluctantly.

Akki caught up with Jakkin. "Who are they?" she asked. "Who was in the copter?"

"And why are they here? Were they looking for us or just flying by?" Jakkin countered.

Questions, like little scurrying animals, rushed back and forth across their bridged minds. The dragons broke through with their own questions about food. They cared little about the copter now that it was out of sight.

Jakkin shrugged and went back to the cave, emerging with a handful of wort. He shared it out, saving the largest portion for Sssargon.

"Brave Sssargon. Sssargon eats." After his announcements the hatchling rose onto his hind legs and gave a hop that sent him some three feet straight up into the air. He pumped his wings at the same time and took off, rocketing up.

As if on cue, the triplets went after him, throwing themselves over the cliffside to catch different parts of the air current, tumbling and bumping in a kind of midair brawl.

Finally Sssasha stepped to the cliff edge. She moved her long neck up and down, head bobbing, as if she were trying to figure out the winds. Her sendings were rosy bubbles in a slow-moving stream, calm and indecipherable. Then, apparently satisfied, she stepped off the cliff and, after a long, slow fall, unfurled her wings to their fullest with a soft *shushing* and floated to the valley below as if she weighed no more than a feather.

After a minute Jakkin said softly, "They've landed."

"Yes," Akki replied. "And they're grazing. I can hear it too. When they eat, their minds go blank and all I get from them is a kind of quiet chuckling." She laughed. "I wonder if we do that too?"

Jakkin walked away from the cliff's edge and sat back down on his haunches. "Maybe dragons can afford to be mindless, but *we* have to think, Akki."

"About what?" She flipped her braid to the front.

"About the copters and who may be searching for us and—"

"What makes you so sure they're looking for us? They could

be looking for anyone. They might be looking for dragons. Or sightseeing." She shrugged. "It's been months since we 'died.' "

"Who else would they be looking for?"

"Rebels."

"The rebels are in the cities, blowing things up. Why would they come out here? There's nothing to destroy." His tone was bitter. "It has to be us the copter was searching for. The Fedders wouldn't waste a copter on anyone small. Sightseeing, ha! What can *they* see at night? As for dragons, if they want to see dragons, they go to the Pits."

"Are you sure?"

"I'm sure!" Jakkin's mind added a solid exclamation point.

Leaning against the rock face, Akki mused, "If they're looking for us, it can't be the Fedders. What Federation rules did we break?"

"That bomb we were tricked into carrying must have killed a lot of Federation starship crewmen at the Pit," Jakkin said.

"Jakkin, I know you dislike politics, but even you know that we are a Protectorate world, not a member of the Fed Congress. Not yet, anyway. That means the Fedders have no rights here. They're bound by *our* laws. It's the wardens who enforce those laws. If the Federation doesn't like what's going on here, there's only one thing it can do."

"Embargo!" Jakkin said.

"Exactly—embargo. No Fedder ships in and no Austarians out."

Jakkin added grimly, "And no outside bettors for the Pits. No imported metals. No contact with the Federation worlds for fifty years. If that happens, we won't be popular."

Akki laughed, but there was nothing happy in the sound. It was brief and hawking, more like a cough than a laugh.

"Well, it can't be the rebels looking for us, can it?" Jakkin said, as much to order his own thoughts as to ask for an answer. "They don't have copters, unless they've stolen one."

"They'd like to do that, I'm sure," Akki put in.

"But stolen copter or not," Jakkin continued, "why would *they* be looking for us?"

"I could still identify them," Akki said. "At least some of them. At least Number One, the leader of my rebel cell."

A picture of the man who called himself Number One exploded with an orange-red ferocity that startled Jakkin because Akki rarely sent anything that strong. One minute the rebel leader was there in Jakkin's mind, his mustache a parenthesis around a slash of mouth, the next he was gone into a million blood-red pieces all shaped like tears.

Jakkin stood and shook his head vigorously to clear it. "Akki, that doesn't make sense. We've been out here for months and too many things will have changed for the rebels. No one will remember you or care."

"It may seem long to us, but Number One is the sort of man who'd pick at his own scab to keep a wound fresh. And you and I are the only ones who could identify him as the real bomber."

Jakkin looked over at her, his eyes wide. "There were other members of Number One's cell besides you, Akki."

Her answering smile was grim. "Do you honestly think they're still alive? That wasn't his way. He thought we would die in the Pit. If he found out we'd survived that, he'd check until he heard how we 'died' on the mountainside. He'd want to be sure."

Jakkin thought a minute. "Someone must have come back and found . . . they must have discovered Heart's Blood's . . . they must have seen her. . . ."

Akki came over and put her hand on his shoulder. "Say it,

Jakkin. Say it and be done with it. If you never say it, it's not real. Say *Heart's Blood's bones.* Someone must have found her bones and not found ours. Say it."

"I don't have to say it to know it."

"Say it so you can be done with grieving. And done with the guilt."

He moved away from her touch. "I'm not grieving. I'm not feeling guilty." But his mind betrayed him again, for the pictures were all of red dragons lying in horrible bloody parts and a boy with a bloody knife standing beside her. Knowing the sending had reached her, Jakkin turned away and spoke in a low voice. "I didn't cry when my father died under the claws of a feral dragon, though I was just a child when it happened. And I didn't cry a year later when my mother died of overwork and loneliness. I didn't cry when my friend, your father, Sarkkhan, was blown up in the Rokk Pit when it should have been me. And I won't cry now." But his sending turned gray and was shot through with blue tears, speaking a different truth.

Akki used the same quieting tone she used with the hatchlings. "It's all right. It's all right to cry, Jakkin."

He shook his head. "We don't have time for tears. We have to think. Someone knows we're alive and is looking for us."

"They may know we're alive, but they don't know everything," Akki said. "They don't know how we've changed. How we can see and hear with dragons' eyes and ears. How we can talk to dragons and each other with sendings. How we can survive the cold of Dark After."

Jakkin nodded slowly.

"And they don't know that we're living here!" Akki said triumphantly.

"*Here* is where we shouldn't be. Fewmets, Akki, why didn't

we see that before? It's been crazy to stay so close . . . so close
. . ." His voice stuttered off again, though his mind sent a picture of the mountain landscape broken into shards, the pieces
looking remarkably like the bones of a dragon.

"You're right," Akki said. "If they look in Golden's Cave or in
the Lookout or here . . . why there's no way anyone is going to
believe dragons made those cups." She gestured toward the cave.

"Or the braided vines," Jakkin added. "Or the mattresses."
He looked out over the mountain pass, now hidden by the darkness. Once he'd seen it as a jagged, threatening landscape. Over
the last months he'd come to know its beauty. And how it reminded him of a dragon's necklinks, not only handsome but
essential for defense. He and Akki knew these mountains as no
one else did. They were part of the landscape now. But if the
rebels found them, their lives would be forfeit. If the trackers
were wardens or Fedders, and they were caught—well, there
were worse things than death. Austar had no physical punish-
ment excepting *transportation.* Break the laws a little, and you
were fined. Break the laws a lot, and you were sent offworld,
transported to another of the penal planets where life was even
harsher than on the tamed Austar. Ice planets like Sedna or
water planets like Lir, where the voices of dragons and the color
patterns would be gone forever.

"Jakkin, please don't do this." Akki's hands were pressed to
her head. "Please talk to me. All I'm getting from you are sendings of windstorms and fire, snowstorms and storms at sea. That
may be good enough for the dragons, but I need words as well."

"Words? All right, then, how about these words—we're leaving. Now. We'll take jars of berries and Boil but leave everything
else."

"Fine," Akki said, her voice hushed. "We can find other

caves. Better ones." Her tone was cheery, but the picture from
her mind was of empty, cheerless rooms.

Suddenly Jakkin wished she had disagreed and put up a fight.
He wished she'd come up with an argument to make them stay.
Yet he knew the decision to leave was the right one. Then why
did he feel so bad?

"It's all right, Jakkin," Akki said. She threw her arms around
him.

He broke away angrily. "Lizard waste, Akki. How can I be
strong when every little doubt or fear broadcasts itself to you. I
hate it!"

Akki turned away, biting her lip and letting a stray apology
wind into his mind. He fought the sending for a long, bitter
moment, but at last accepted it, twined it with a blue braid, and
let the two colors slowly fade as he walked back into the cave.

Using carry-slings fashioned from woven weeds, they packed
the jars, carefully separating them with mattress grass. They
corked two jars of Boil with pieces of wood Jakkin shaved down
to fit. Then he helped Akki slip the smaller sling over her shoulders. She in turn helped him take up the heavier load.

Besides the food, they packed Jakkin's knife, the old book of
dragon stories Golden had given them, and a spear Jakkin had
made by sharpening a dragon femur he'd found in one of the
lower caves. They knew they'd have to browse for other food,
but they were both expert scavengers by now. In the mountains
berries, mushrooms, and skkagg for Boil were common all year
around. If they were lucky, in the higher meadows they might
find lizard eggs and even kkrystals, the translucent six-legged
insects that lived in lizard nests. A kkrystal dipped in beaten egg
and crisped over a fire was delicious. Insects had no sendings, or

at least none they could hear, and so Jakkin and Akki felt no remorse about eating them.

Akki walked around the cave one last time, as if memorizing it. There was so little there, yet it had taken them months to make it seem like home.

"We might never see it again," she whispered.

"If we don't leave soon, we might never see *anything* again," Jakkin answered. Quite deliberately he shaped a picture of a copter in his mind, a blood-red copter winging toward them. There were three men in it, one wearing a Fedder flight cap, one a warden's hat, and the other had a mustache over a slash of mouth.

"If we don't leave soon, I might change my mind," Akki added.

Jakkin was glad she had said it, and he worked very hard to keep the same thought out of any of his own sendings.

Walking into the false dawn, they scarcely felt the bitter cold.

5

They walked up the path for an hour in silence, both intent on masking their minds, the only sounds the occasional rattling of a loose pebble rolling down the mountainside or the *pick-buzz* of flikka wings. Then the path widened and made a great turn and they found themselves in the Upper Meadows, a plateau some three kilometers across.

Even in the dark Jakkin knew the place. He did not need to see the gray-green furze cover broken by the mounds of berry bushes to recognize it. He knew there was a cliff face on one side that sat like the crown of a hat on the plateau's brim. The place was engraved forever in his mind. It was here that Heart's Blood had died for them. He drew in a deep breath, and when he let it out again it sounded like a sigh.

Akki reached over and touched his hand.

"I finally found a path, you know," she said. "It's through one of the caves. Well, not exactly a cave, but more like a tunnel."

He didn't answer, but they both had the same awful thought leaping in lightning strokes from mind to mind: If they had found the tunnel those many months ago, Heart's Blood need not have died.

"Close your eyes, Jakkin, and I'll lead you past."

He knew she meant past the remains, the bones, all that was left of his beautiful red dragon. Obediently he closed his eyes and held out his hand. At her touch his mind replayed the final scene when Heart's Blood, smoke streaming from her nose slits, had risen in a hindfoot stand. Front legs raking the air, she had taken three shots fired at them from the near dark. One had struck the rocks right above her uplifted head. One had shattered the cliff beside Akki. And the third had raised a bloody flower on Heart's Blood's throat. He recalled how she fell, slowly, endlessly, forever.

Akki pulled him by the hand, whispering encouragements while he concentrated on not crying. When she stopped suddenly he almost fell over her.

"Bend your head," she said, "and walk forward."

Shuffling along, he felt the cool dampness of a tunnel surround him, like a dash at the end of a long sentence. He opened his eyes.

"The bones are outside," Akki said quietly. "But that's all they are—just bones. Not ghosts or demons or—"

"They're Heart's Blood's bones," Jakkin said. "And we both know it."

She nodded. There was nothing more she could say.

The tunnel was short and opened onto a steep pathway where strange half-shadows played on the path under a sky lightening into gray dawn. For several more hours they climbed, winding upward without speaking.

Jakkin could feel Akki's longing for the caves they'd left, caves that were now only minor pocks in the landscape. That longing crossed his mind as an endless gray sending, but he didn't let her know how much she had let her feeling leak out, for it began to occur to him that one way to become private was to respect another's privacy. Instead he hummed monotonously to disguise his reaction.

When they reached a sharp switchback they both rested for a moment, drawing in deep breaths that slowly synchronized. Akki leaned against the rock wall and made no move to go on, but Jakkin stepped around the turn, doggedly determined to continue.

Around the bend he saw that the way flattened and then widened into an unexpected barren arena, as large as a minor dragon Pit the carved-out bowl of a mountaintop.

"Akki, come see this!" he called.

She rounded the bend and was as surprised as he.

"I've never made it this far before or seen anything like this," she said.

Jakkin scouted the base of the eastern slope and Akki the western. Since they'd come up over the southern rim, they had to find some alternate descent or else just go back the way they had come. But the best they found was a small handscrabble and rock-strewn trail running up the northwestern side.

"Maybe it widens later on," Jakkin said cautiously.

Akki shrugged, her mind a careful blank.

The path did widen after about a hundred steps up the slope but only slightly. What was worse was that at every turning there seemed to have been a rockslide. Great plugs of granite blocked the narrow, twisting trail and at each one they had to scramble hand over hand over the rocks. Jakkin went first, after giving his pack to Akki. Once on top, he leaned down and took both packs from her, hauling them to the top, then sliding them down the far side. Then he extended a hand down to Akki and helped her up. It was slow, exhausting, sweaty work, and they didn't make good time.

Sitting atop the third pile of rocks, Akki took a deep breath. "How many more of these do you think?"

Jakkin shook his head, too winded to talk.

A moment later Akki managed another sentence. "Couldn't we call the hatchlings in? After all, Sssargon says he's our eyes. Let *them* tell us what's ahead."

"Good idea," Jakkin said. "Why didn't we think of that earlier?" He shaped a careful sending of red and gold flags flapping in the wind, wound about with his signature color of green. He kept it quiet at first so as not to hurt Akki's head and after a while felt her blue braid winding around the green. They broadcast the sending as loudly as they dared until Akki's part of it began to waver and she put her hand to her head. Still there was no answer.

"They must be miles away," Akki whispered, rubbing her temples.

"Or just not answering," Jakkin added.

"Like babies."

He nodded. "Big babies."

They both laughed and the ache in their heads bled away.

"Wouldn't it make life simpler if we could ride a dragon?" Jakkin said at last.

"That's impossible."

"I knew you'd say that. But wouldn't it be nice if we *could.*"

"You *know* that any extra weight on a dragon's back presses against the flight muscles and—"

"Anatomy lessons?" he asked innocently, referring to her medical studies in The Rokk.

"Oh, you worm pile, you're just egging me on." She tried to look grim but started to giggle and, as if to tease him back, formed very graphic sendings of the kinds of wounds dragon scales inflict on the inner thighs of any humans foolish enough to sit on them. When she saw Jakkin flinch Akki grinned broadly. "Now *there's* a real anatomy lesson," she said. "All the muscles laid bare. I had to stitch up a number of drunken bonders for trying such stupid things on walking dragons."

Quite deliberately, Jakkin stuck his tongue out at her and was surprised—and embarrassed—at how much better it made him feel.

"So, we're even now," Akki said. "And I could use something to drink." She slid down the rocks to the sling packs below and took out a jar of Boil. Taking a deep draft, she passed the jar up to Jakkin. He made a face, more for her amusement than for real, and drank his share. Even Boil tasted good after hours of climbing.

"What would happen, do you suppose," Akki mused, "if we tried to clear a path instead of climbing over each and every rock?"

"It'd take forever," Jakkin said, wiping his hand across his mouth. "And time is important. It'll be day soon, and the copter will probably be back."

Akki nodded. "We'd probably start an avalanche anyway."

"And alert every wild dragon around," Jakkin added.

"Bury villages too," Akki said, smiling, her ironic tone clear in the words. At the same time her sending was of an idyllic picture of a peaceful village.

Without meaning to, Jakkin sent back a scene of the same village with a series of small blue-gray people, shadows of shadows in an endless line, standing in front of the houses.

Akki touched his arm. "Are you lonely?" she asked.

Immediately a fall of rocks buried the shadow people and their village. "I have you, Akki," Jakkin said. "And the hatchlings when they bother to answer. How can I be lonely?"

Akki corked the jar and banged her fist on the cork. "That's what I asked," she said. "And you answered me with another question."

They walked on until the path made a particularly bad turning, with only a foot's width between the cliffside and a steep drop. Their slings overbalanced them precariously.

Akki, who was in front, clung to the cliff and moved one foot at a time, then disappeared around the bend. Jakkin heard her cry out, "Look! Oh, Jakkin, look!"

He couldn't move quickly, and his heart was pounding madly by the time he'd come around the same precarious bend. Then he saw what had so astonished her. After the turn the path was nothing but jumbled rockfall for a few feet and then, below that, an unexpected meadow covered with deep purple gorse and dotted with bright green trees.

Akki slid down the rockfall, but Jakkin, conscious of the jars of Boil in his pack, picked his way carefully.

"One, two . . . three. Look, Jakkin, there are seven spikkas."

The trees, with their crowns of spiked leaves, were unmistakable, though they were shorter and spindlier than valley spikkas. They all leaned toward the eastern slope at a comical angle.

Jakkin counted quickly. "You're right—seven—and over there

a few smaller ones sprouting." He pointed to the far edge of the meadow where the gorse ended suddenly in a sharp, spectacular drop. "How could spikkas grow so high up? And look how they lean."

"They lean because of the prevailing winds," Akki said. "And they're up here because dragons fly."

Jakkin snorted. "Of course dragons fly."

"When they fly the seeds of the trees often stick to their underbellies or go through them undigested and out in the fewmets, and if they land here and—"

"No lessons," Jakkin said. He smiled. "It wasn't that kind of question."

Smiling back, she nodded. "No lessons."

"It's morning and getting warm. We should rest here, under the trees. They may lean, but their crowns are full enough to hide us from copters overhead. We can look for food later on." He wasn't afraid to admit his exhaustion, and besides—he reminded himself—Akki had probably already read it in his thoughts.

Running over to the closest spikka, Akki dropped her sling pack and began to dance around the tree. Then she stopped, looked up at the leaves as if counting them, and shook her head. "Not this one. We, my friend, are going to sleep under the prettiest one in the copse."

"Some copse," Jakkin said. "Seven spindly trees widely spaced is not a copse."

"Who says?"

"I say."

"Where is it written?"

"Here!" He pointed to his head and sent her a very vivid

picture of a book with illuminated words spelling out in fiery colors *7 TREES NOT A COPSE.*

Laughing, Akki picked up her pack and walked over to what was, without a doubt, the tallest and handsomest tree of the seven. She dropped her pack and flopped down under it, signaling Jakkin with her hand.

He walked toward her humming an old nursery melody.

Akki took up the melody and added words.

> *Night is coming,*
> *See the moons;*
> *Softly thrumming*
> *Dragon tunes.*
>
> *Sky above is*
> *Filled with laughter,*
> *Dragons care not*
> *For Dark After.*
>
> *Dawn . . .*

"*We come, we come, we come,*" the sending was clear.

And then, from farther away, almost an echo, came the sendings of the two largest hatchlings.

"*Sssargon feeds now. Sssargon comes soon.*"

And then Sssasha's languid message. "*I ride the winds. I come after.*"

Turning on her side, Akki mumbled something.

"What?" His voice was a whisper.

Out loud, in imitation of Sssargon's sendings, Akki announced in a deep voice, "Akki sleeps."

Jakkin laughed and curled up by her side. "We'll both sleep

now and eat at dusk. Then we'll find a way down from here when the moons begin to rise. It will be much safer that way."

Akki's only answer was a light, bubbly snore. Jakkin was still trying to figure out whether it was fake or real when he slipped into sleep himself.

6

In the middle of a dream in which he and a great red dragon were lazing by the side of a stream, Jakkin stirred uneasily. A dark cloud entered the dream, raining drops of fire onto the sand. He woke to an overpowering stench, a landscape in his head as barbed and as angry as any he had ever felt, and a steady babble of dragon voices churning across the picture.

"Sssargon kill. Sssargon save."

"Help. Help. Help."

"Do not move. Do not thrash. Help comes."

Jakkin leaped up and looked around, sleep still lapping at the edges of his sight. Akki, sitting on the ground, was as puzzled.

Then in front of the first of the rising moons they saw their hatchlings flying, four of them, in a tight circle. They were backwinging, tails linked, holding up the fifth, whose wing drooped strangely. Around that circle was another circle of fliers, an attack force of silent winged shadows with long snaky necks and blunted heads.

"Drakk," breathed Jakkin.

"Up this high?" Akki's voice was strained. "I thought they ranged the lowlands."

"They roost in trees. In spikkas . . ." He looked up the trunk of the tree warily but could see only the jagged teeth of the leaves. His hand went quickly to the knife on the braided belt. Then he shook his head. "Useless," he muttered. "Useless against one drakk, and look—there's a whole pod of them."

"Hush. Listen."

Jakkin tuned in on the ring of dragons. Beyond their babbling he could feel the heavy dark thoughts of the drakk. Unlike smaller lizards, whose minds were uniformly pale pink or gray, the drakk's sendings were sharp: blue-black, barbed, eternally hungry. They fed on the fear of a wounded dragon long before they stripped the meat from its flesh. The pipings of a dragon hatchling roused them to a frenzy. And one of the triplets was piping its fear.

Akki whispered, "I thought drakk hunted alone."

"So did I," Jakkin said. "But these are mountain drakk."

"That awful drakk smell," Akki added.

The smell. Jakkin turned. That smell meant that somewhere nearby was a wounded or dead drakk. He looked below the ring of dragons and, by the edge of the meadow, saw a dark shape he had not noticed before, broken upon the stones.

"There," he said, pointing. "The dragons have already gotten one."

Akki nodded. "How can we help them? As long as they're up in the air, what can we do?"

"Lend me your mind. Think as I think. They have a bit of training. Maybe enough. Fewmets, I wish I'd taken more time with them. But Sssasha is pretty big and listens well. And

Sssargon is nearly full-grown." He reached out and Akki put her hand in his, for touching seemed to strengthen a sending.

Concentrating, Jakkin sent a message to the dragons. *"At my signal, breathe out fire."* He knew that, large as they were, they were still young, and he'd had no supply of burnwort to help stoke the flames. Of the five only Sssasha and Sssargon could even trickle smoke yet. But he also knew that fear and anger sometimes triggered a fiery display. Perhaps a flame or two would be enough of a surprise to move the ring of drakk back.

"Wishes fill no bags," Akki reminded him. Then she squeezed his hand as if in apology.

The bit of nursery wisdom focused him. He nodded. *"At my signal,"* he reminded the dragons. *"Breathe fire and then at the next, drop down to me. All at once."*

He repeated the instructions twice. He felt sure that the drakk, with their wordless, dark minds, couldn't understand the plan.

Above them, dipping and rising against the first pale moon, the two circles continued their deadly dance. Thrust, retreat, thrust, retreat. Below them, at the ridge, the second moon's aura was just beginning to show. The drakk ring tightened like a noose. Guided by the dragon smell and the constant piping of the wounded Tri, the nearsighted monsters closed in.

"When I count to three," Jakkin said to Akki, "think about the hottest flames you can. It will help them concentrate, and flame is something they know instinctively. The moment the drakk move back, think—*drop!*" He handed Akki his knife and picked up the femur spear, which he'd left lying against the spikka.

Akki held the knife before her and bit her lip.

"One . . ." Jakkin whispered aloud.

Akki nodded.

"Two . . ." He could feel her tension.

"Three. Fire!" Jakkin roared aloud and Akki screamed with
him. They sent picture after picture of blazing firebombs and
roaring flames, shouting and waving their arms about as an
added distraction.

In response, Sssargon trickled some smoke from his nose,
enough to make the sky around them hazy. But it was Sssasha,
placid Sssasha, who suddenly flared out with a tongue of flame as
long as a mature fighter's. It licked at the face of the nearest
drakk, which banked out of the circle, hissing wildly, and crashed
onto the rocks below.

Sssargon tried again. His smoke forced the nearest drakk to
blink its near-dead white eyes and back away. Sssasha managed
another fire flash. It raked the side of a drakk that had not been
pushed back by the smoke. The drakk turned and the circle was
broken.

"Now drop!" Akki and Jakkin screamed, their minds linking as
one.

The ring of dragons plummeted to the ground, frantically
backwinging at the last moment so as not to crash and further
injure the wounded Tri.

No sooner had they dropped than Jakkin instructed them,
"Form a ring on the ground. Now—hindfoot rise." He sent the
kind of controlled messages he'd used when guiding a fighting
dragon in the Pit. Only this was not for gold, but for life, so
there was an added edge of fright in his sending.

Sssargon understood at once and Sssasha was not far behind.
Even little Tri-ssskkette, the wounded one, tried to stand, front
claws raised and waiting.

For a moment Jakkin closed his eyes, remembering Heart's

Blood. He felt tears beginning in the corners of his eyes. Blinking them back, he forced himself to look, but his grip on the spear tightened.

The lead drakk and the flame-racked second dived.

Jakkin flashed out with the sharpened spear, catching the front drakk in the head above the eye. He did not pierce its hide, but he jarred it enough to disrupt its perfect dive and Sssasha ripped its neck open with her claws. Then she grabbed the drakk in her mouth and flung it with such force, it tumbled to the edge of the cliff.

The second drakk banked sharply and winged away.

The fallen drakk lay on its side, still except for the pulsing sensor organs on the underside of its wings. Its malevolent, blind snake eyes shuttered and unshuttered rapidly. Viscous blood oozed from its neck.

Akki ran over to the cliff's edge and picked up an enormous rock. Holding it over her head, she walked purposefully to the drakk, ready to drop the stone on the dying beast. She bent over it and Jakkin ran up behind her and yanked her back.

At that moment the drakk's hind claws razored through the air just where Akki's legs had been seconds before.

"It's not dead!" she cried out in horror.

"It's dead," Jakkin said. "Or near enough. But even dead it'll make a final fatal pass, a kind of reflex, because of those sensors." He pointed to the fleshy sensors. They were still pulsing. "Didn't you study *that* in your anatomy lessons?" he asked.

"I never studied drakk," she said softly.

"Someone at the nursery told me he knew a man whose leg was nearly severed in two by a very dead drakk."

Akki shivered and let the rock fall.

Hot, foul-smelling drakk blood oozed onto the gorse.

"Last time," mused Jakkin, "the smell of that blood made me sick."

"Last time you weren't part dragon," Akki said, but her voice was strange, and Jakkin suddenly realized it was because she was holding her nose.

Sssargon walked stiff-legged over to the dead drakk and, using only the tip of his tail, poked and prodded it gingerly, waiting for a response. When there was none he pushed the drakk slowly—from the backside only—through the ground cover and over the edge of the cliff. When it landed, after a long fall, Sssasha sent a chuckling thought into Jakkin's head.

"Splat!!!" Then she turned her attention to helping Tri-sssk-kette, slowly licking the torn wing. When the wound was clean she swiveled her great head toward Akki. *"Fix?"*

Akki smiled weakly and went back to the spikka. Her sling pack lay under the tree. In one of the jars were the remains of her medkit. She whispered to Jakkin, "I hope the needles I have are strong enough for dragon skin." Threading the needle, she went to work. Her small, careful stitches patchworked the flesh and scale feathers that had been torn. "See," she said to Jakkin, "luckily the *bande dominus,* the big wing bone here, is untouched. Otherwise she would have been in real trouble."

Jakkin nodded, muttering under his breath, *"Bande dominus."*

After a few minutes, except for the strange nobbiness of the thread, the wing looked as good as new.

"No more sleeping under trees," said Jakkin. "There are still a number of drakk there. And since they usually fly in a straight trajectory"—he hesitated—"they probably nest right here in the meadow. In the top of one of these spikkas."

Sssargon's anger suddenly forced its way through to them in

red-hot splashes. *"Sssargon fight. Sssargon flames."* And to everyone's amazement he shot a spearhead of flame out half a meter.

"Sssargon has lousy timing," said Akki, but she reached out and scratched him under the chin.

"Thou brave worm," Jakkin said, unconsciously falling into the elevated formal language that Pit trainers used with their dragons.

Sssargon preened under their attention, oblivious of the ironic undertones. He even sent a wilder thought to them: *"Sssargon kill. Kill all. Sssargon flames once more."*

"Worm," warned Jakkin, "we can't be running off to fight now."

"Yes, brave Sssargon," said Akki, holding up the medkit. "We have little thread left for sewing up thy mighty wings."

"And only one small knife and one small spear and . . ."

Sssargon's fiery reply shot through them. He did not understand, nor did he *want* to understand, human reasoning. He wanted blood and earth and air and fire. When Akki tried to send a soothing gray cloud to cover his burning landscape, he shook it off, pumped his wings, and leaped into the air. They could feel the backwind as he flipped to the left and flew out over the valley, his defiance screaming into their minds.

"Lizard waste," shouted Jakkin after him. Turning to Akki, he said, "I've never had a dragon act like this."

"You're used to nursery dragons, trained and pampered. These hatchlings are wild."

"Well, they weren't born wild," Jakkin said.

"His temper will burn off up there in the sky. He's a bit put out, I think, that Sssasha was the great hero of the fight when he thought he should be," she said, putting the medkit back in her pack. "Reminds me of a boy I once knew." She smiled.

"Not funny," said Jakkin, but he couldn't keep from smiling back at her. "However, *that's* a dragon long overdue for some hard training."

"You're not exactly the picture of a trainer now."

He looked down at his shorts, the dirty remnants of his white trainer's suit. They were patched and repatched, the earlier, crisper darns done by Akki, the later ones, his own coarse handiwork. "Well," he admitted, "I guess I don't *look* like one. But I still know training. And a certain amount of discipline is necessary, as today proves. If we're all to survive, we have to find ways of working together."

Akki was silent and her thoughts blank.

"Fewmets, Akki, wasn't that the first lesson we learned in the nursery? Isn't that what our grandfathers learned when they were dumped on Austar?"

Akki's voice was very quiet. "I thought you said the first and best lesson was *I fill my bag myself.*" She touched his chest where the leather bag used to hang, the bag that signaled to all the world that he was a bonder, the bag he'd filled with gold enough to buy his freedom.

"We aren't wearing bondbags anymore."

"No, and we haven't for some time, Jakkin."

"Then why are we arguing?" Jakkin asked. "We don't have time for arguments. We've got to get away from this meadow. Now."

"Now, now, now. All of a sudden everything is *now* with you. And besides, we aren't arguing, Jakkin. We're discussing things, like sophisticated folk do."

"Like city folk?" asked Jakkin. "Is that what you learned the year you lived in The Rokk with the rebels?"

"I learned to talk about things that matter with Golden and

with Dr. Henkky," Akki said. "I learned to talk out my feelings before they got so big . . . oh, never mind, Jakkin. How can you understand? You'd rather send to dragons."

"Akki, that's not true." But she had turned away. He picked up his sling and stood there, his mouth empty of words but his mind swirling and confused, and Akki, he was sure, heard it all.

7

Without speaking to each other, they walked the rim of the gorse meadow looking for a new path down the mountain. Their feet kicked up insects that chittered and flew away. Keeping pace with them were the four hatchlings, who trampled the purple ground cover with their massive feet.

Sssasha kept checking the skies, though it wasn't clear whether she was looking for more drakk or trying to find the sulking Sssargon. Unlike humans, dragons sent only what they wanted to send unless they were in the middle of a fight.

Tri-ssskkette's sendings kept breaking into jagged little markers of pain and, with the other two echoing her every mental whimper, it made concentration difficult for them all. Jakkin tried sending calming thoughts to the triplet, but nothing seemed to work until Akki began a light show of raucous, bumpy colors that finally took the hatchling's mind off her wounds.

Jakkin turned to Akki and drew in a deep breath. "Thanks," he whispered at last.

Akki shrugged. "Some patients need a lot of sympathy and

some need a lot of distracting." She stopped for a moment, seemed to calculate, then added, "Dr. Henkky taught me that."

"She's a smart lady," Jakkin said. It seemed to make peace between them and Jakkin smiled with relief.

They continued to walk the meadow edge, but it was like looking over the rim of a bowl.

"I don't see any paths but the one we came up," Akki said as they circled a second time. She rubbed the side of her head. The light show was beginning to wear her down.

"Well, we can't go back that way," Jakkin said. "Not after all this."

"Without a path, we can't go anywhere else."

"What do you want us to do?" Jakkin asked. "Sit here and wait for the drakk to return? Or the copter?" His voice was overloud.

"Jakkin, *I'm* not the enemy," Akki said. "Don't yell at me."

He was about to apologize, feeling stupid about losing his temper, when Sssasha sent a picture of a cave into his head. The cave had a long, winding thread of light running end to end.

Jakkin shook his head to clear it, but Sssasha's calling came again, steady, insistent. "In?" Jakkin asked. "You want us to find a cave and go in? That's no real solution. Fine for a night, maybe. Drakk don't go in caves. And copters won't find us there. But it won't last forever. We need a way down this mountain."

"Maybe she means a cave like the tunnel," Akki broke in.

"Maybe," Jakkin said. "But I haven't seen any caves, have you?"

Akki shook her head. The rock face had been solid.

Turning in a deliberate, lumbering manner, Sssasha headed toward the rock face beyond them. On a hunch, Jakkin ran after her, and then, with a burst of speed, reached the wall of rock

first. The cliff was veined with a dark material and rose straight
up, without handholds. At the bottom, where it met the
meadow, instead of the ever-present gorse there was a thicket of
prickly caught-ums. With his spear Jakkin gingerly parted strand
after strand of the tangle. It seemed a hopeless task.

Sssasha moved slightly to the right and stared at the rock.

"Here," said Akki, catching up to them. "Try here, where
she's looking."

Jakkin picked at the caught-ums with the spear and on the
fifth try he spotted a low, dark hole. Akki carefully held apart the
nearer vines, holding her fingers above and below the caught-um
thorns while Jakkin used the spear to pull apart the rest of the
thicket.

"How could she know it was there?" Akki asked.

"Maybe she saw it when she was flying? From above?" His
answers seemed more like questions. "Or maybe dragons can,
you know, sense caves?"

"Do you mean this one?" asked Akki, sending the thought
simultaneously to Sssasha.

Sssasha's answer was another picture, this time of a close,
pulsing darkness that reminded both Jakkin and Akki of the egg
chamber where they had been sheltered and changed.

Jakkin looked again at the wall and the low opening, then
turned to the dragon. But Sssasha, sensing some kind of signal
that the humans could not read, was already pumping her wings
in preparation for flight. The three smaller hatchlings fanned the
air in imitation. Even Tri-ssskkette, her wounded wing stuttering
in the small eddies, managed to rise up and hover for a moment
over the bushes. The wind from the four pair of wings caused
the caught-ums to sway, as if great waves were passing through.

Then the hatchlings rose higher, banked in formation, and, led by Sssasha, disappeared over the top of the cliff.

"Stop!" Akki shouted. "Come back."

But the dragons were too far off to hear, and they ignored her sendings, even when Jakkin joined her. Soon they were out of sight.

Dropping to a crouch before the thicket, Akki said, "That's the first time they've *all* disobeyed." Then she added softly, "I sure hope those stitches hold." Hand up over her eyes, she continued to stare at the spot in the sky where the dragons had disappeared.

Jakkin examined the cave entrance. "I guess that's our only choice," he said, pointing.

Akki turned back and nodded.

They rounded up their packs, making sure nothing but the trampled gorse gave evidence of their stay there. Then, carefully, so as not to scratch their hands, they pulled apart enough of the intertwining branches of the caught-ums, hooking them on to peripheral strands until they had a clear if narrow path leading into the cave.

When they reached the rock Jakkin turned and, using his spear, unlocked the knot behind them. The brambles sprang back, once again obscuring the cave.

"No one could possibly know we're in here," Jakkin said, his mind sending its own version of a gate slammed shut.

They were cold the moment they entered the cave. It was colder than any cave they had ever been in before, as if it were fed by some great belly of wind from below. And there was a strange hollow echo in it that gave them back breath for breath. Jakkin pulled his gray-white shirt out of the sling and put it on.

"I don't like it," Akki said, shivering. Parts of her voice, terribly distorted, came back to them from the black walls: *I . . . ikeit . . . ikeit . . . ikeit.* "It's not—not welcoming, like our other caves. There's something *ugly* here. I don't know what it is, but I feel it."

Although Jakkin didn't answer, his own mistrust linked with hers.

They reached out and grabbed hands, as if touch alone could warm them, and together began to inch forward into the cave. It was dark inside, and though their gift of dragon sight usually meant they could see colors in the dark, the cave was void of any light. It was a darkness that matched the cold.

Rounding a bend, they found themselves in a secondary cave with a ceiling high enough so they could stand upright. Ahead was a faint gleaming that cast a grayish light on the shadowy walls. Instinctively they went toward the light, their fingers twined together.

The glow seemed to come from a pile of sticks stacked up so high, the top reached the cave ceiling.

Akki reached out with her free hand and touched one of the protruding sticks cautiously. "It's cold," she said. "And porous."

Jakkin put his hand on another stick. "That's bone," he said.

Akki looked more closely, horrified. "You're right," she said. She touched a different bone. "Oh, my God," she said. "Jakkin, look! Femur, fibula, humerus, another femur, tibia, and these little ones. They're caudal vertebrae." She went up and down the stack, touching the bones and naming them, until she added unnecessarily, "Dragon bones." The echo in the cave mocked her horror, whispering in return, *Ones . . . ones . . . ones.*

Despite the cold, Jakkin felt a fine film of sweat on his palms as Akki counted out the bones. It took a moment more for him to get out the question that seemed to be echoing inside him. "What . . ." he began, his voice cracking, "what can be big enough to eat this many dragons?" He hesitated, then mused aloud, "Not drakk."

"What would be big enough to strip the bones—and then neat enough to stack them?" Akki added. "Stack them in an intricate, interlocking pattern?"

"We're leaving," Jakkin said. "Now."

The echo added its own mocking note.

They backed out of the dark, high chamber and reentered the lower room. The cave mouth, even shuttered with the caught-ums, suddenly seemed to blaze with light and they started toward the opening.

A strange chuffing sound leaked through the thorny thicket and into the cave. Jakkin crouched by the cave mouth and listened. Something whirred around the clearing and settled in.

"Copter!" he sent to Akki, not daring to speak aloud or stir up the cave's echoes again, even though with the noise the copter was making, he knew he'd never be heard. Carefully he checked that the caught-ums were securely laced over the opening. As far as he could tell, they showed no evidence of entry.

"We have disappeared," Akki sent back, forming a picture of a barred door. Jakkin recognized it as the sending he had envisioned earlier when they had first come into the cave. But there was a strange darker color in Akki's sending that might have been either grim satisfaction—or fear.

They edged backward till they came again to the bend. Fearfully they rounded it and huddled together against the wall in the chamber of bones. Akki's hand found Jakkin's and he was relieved that her hand was as moist as his own.

Two or three shouting voices reached them, any meaning lost

through the filter of brush and stone. The cave echoed their own heavy breathing until it seemed as if the dark itself was filled with fearful respirations.

"Did we leave anything out there, anything they might recognize as ours?" Jakkin whispered into Akki's ear.

She was a long time answering. At last a quiet sending reached into his mind. It was of a landscape that, except for a few sketchy trees, was barren.

Jakkin wondered suddenly if the dead drakk puzzled the searchers. They could hardly miss it. The smell alone would warn them. He was glad he'd stopped Akki from beating in the drakk's head with a rock. Surely the searchers—whether they were rebels, wardens, or Fedders—would realize that the drakk had been killed by dragons. And Sssasha's heavy tread on the gorse should have wiped out any sign of their smaller feet.

One last shout came to them, then the whir of the copter.

A weak sending suddenly came through, a picture of a copter with the copse and mountain foreshortened. The copter in the sending rose up from the gorse and headed in a southerly direction.

"Gone," came Sssasha's sending, ending with a quiet, bubbling *"Good!"*

"Yes, good," Jakkin said aloud, and sighed deeply. The sudden echo startled him, *Ooood . . . ood . . . ooood.* It seemed to go on and on, finally dying off with a hissing, echoed sigh. He crept forward to the cave mouth and turned his head to see Akki in the darkness. "Come on," he said. "We can get out of here now."

"Wait," Akki said. "I hear something else. Not the copter. Not our own echoes. Something else."

When the tickling echo of her words had died away, Jakkin

listened, too, straining into the colorless cold. He didn't know what to expect, perhaps the sound of lizards scrabbling on overhead ledges, perhaps the breath of dragons, perhaps whatever large predator had eaten the dragons and stacked their bones on the floor. What he heard instead was a sending, teasing and gray, as insistent as a trainer's command.

"Come. Come. COME. COME."

There was something else beneath the sending and around it, a wilder note, like singing.

Without willing it, he crawled back into the cave of bones, then stood and reached for Akki's hand once more. They walked around the pile of bones. Behind it was a tunnel.

"COME. COME. COME. COME."

The singing was higher now, like the piping of a flute.

Will-less, as if in a spell out of Golden's book of dragon lore, they plunged hand in hand into the tunnel, which closed around them, a narrow, stifling, winding tube.

8

After the first few turns they had to drop hands, needing both to feel along the sides of the tunnel. Though the sides were cold, damp, even slippery to the touch, it was the grayness that amazed Jakkin the most. Outside, when the moons set and Dark After was complete, there was always enough light to make colors. In the bone room the bones had lent a strange glow to the cave, and then the phosphorescent fungi on the walls of the tunnel had allowed them some further shades. But this part of the cave seemed just an endless gray shadow land that was more depressing and frightening than black night before the *change* had ever been.

Jakkin could not help himself, and his feelings broadcast to Akki. But when her own fear pulsed back at him, he felt only relief, as if her fear excused his. He relaxed into a yawn.

"I'm sleepy," Akki said just as he yawned. Her mind babbled at him, suddenly childlike, sending quiet little pictures of gray water and gray waves. "I think I'm going to sit down." It reminded Jakkin of one of Sssargon's pronouncements.

That seemed right—sitting down. They'd been walking hours,

with little sleep. Jakkin struggled against another yawn, and when Akki sagged against him, he put his arms around her and let his own knees bend slowly.

Just then the strange faraway sending began again, steady and insistent, like an alien heartbeat.

"*COME. COME.*" Then a pause and a repeat. "*COME. COME.*" Entwining it, like a dark vine around a bright pillar of light, was another voice that sang to them a wordless, soothing song.

"Forward," Jakkin mumbled. "We've got to go forward." He yanked Akki up with him, wondering only slightly why his voice sounded a register higher, childlike.

They plodded ahead, and when the tunnel's air got close Akki dropped her pack. Jakkin bent to retrieve it, dragged it after him for a few steps, and then let it fall.

"*COME. COME.*"

The tunnel flared open again and little flecks of light, like the wild fire of a fighting dragon's eye, seemed to wink at them from the walls.

"*COME. COME.*"

Akki shivered and Jakkin put his arm around her. He could feel the sweat through her shirt. She stumbled, went down on one knee, out of the protection of his arm, and gave a sharp cry. When she stood up she held something white in her hand.

"Our neat bone-stacker is getting sloppy," Jakkin said, running a finger over the top of the bone. It was a *bande dominus,* the large knobby bone from a dragon's wing.

It provoked no laugh from Akki, who began to shiver again.

Jakkin's foot kicked something that clattered away in the darkness. He got to his knees to try to find it by its gleam, but there were no telltale white patches anywhere on the tunnel floor and he guessed it had fallen into a ditch or ricocheted around a bend. He lifted his head suddenly and realized that the singing and the command had stopped. It felt as if a headache that had long and mysteriously plagued him had disappeared. He shook his head.

"This is crazy," he said aloud, his voice back to its normal pitch. "What are we doing here? We have to find our way back and mark our passage or we'll be lost in here forever."

Akki grunted her agreement.

They turned, heading back the way they had come. With his head clear of the mental message, Jakkin found he could see a bit more. The gray was *not* complete, lit as it was by flickering jewels in the wall. He reached out to touch one, and when his hand came close to it, it winked out as if it were an eye, but where the eye had been was only a pinpoint of icy air.

He caught his breath and stumbled on, not mentioning this discovery to Akki, since he wasn't sure what it meant. Perhaps the mountain was only a shell and these tunnels were close to the outside. Perhaps there was some more sinister meaning. But she was already frightened enough, so he calmed his traitor thoughts and sent a strengthening picture to her instead.

They walked along silently for some time, following the twistings of the tunnel. At last Akki spoke, though Jakkin had already guessed what she wanted to say, her absolute fear having snaked into his mind moments before.

"We're lost, Jakkin. I know it."

"How can you be sure?"

"We haven't stumbled over my pack, have we? We should have come on it long ago. And the path seems to be going down instead of up. If we were in the right tunnel, we would have found the cave opening by now."

He made more soothing sounds, but he knew she was right.

He'd figured it out himself scant moments before, and his mind sent out a confirmation before he could stop it.

Akki sat down on the cold stone and, after a moment of hesitation, Jakkin did the same. For a long time they were silent, their bridged minds sending landscapes of gray despair back and forth, pictures compounded of nervousness and the steady drip-dripping of eroding confidence.

Jakkin forced himself to reach over and pat Akki's shoulder. That touch comforted them both. She moved over and snuggled against him.

And then they heard a sound, a quick scuttering, as if hundreds of tiny feet were coming toward them.

"The bones," Akki whispered. "The monsters of the bone pile."

Into Jakkin's head exploded the picture of that pile magnified by Akki's fear into a mountain of dripping blood, red blood, the first color he had been able to conjure in a long while.

The sound got closer.

They scrambled up, determined to face whatever it was on their feet, and they pressed their backs against the wall as if they could disappear into the resisting stone. Akki was holding her breath on and off. Each time she had to let it out to take another breath there was a tiny explosion of sound that echoed mockingly from the walls. Jakkin tried to slow his own breathing but it seemed to roar out instead, bouncing off the stone. He could feel his heart pounding, too, and that noise was so loud he wondered that there was no answering echo.

And still the slithering, skuttering sound came closer, as if the monster bone-stackers had rounded yet another bend in the tunnel.

Jakkin grabbed Akki's shoulder and she let out a high yip.

"I *know* that sound," he said. "The echoes confused me at first, but I recognize it now."

"What . . . is . . . it?" Akki asked.

"In the nursery," Jakkin said breathlessly. "When we unstalled the dragons and led them through the halls, the hens in heat dragged their tails behind them on the ground and made that shushing sound. That was when we first knew they were ready to mate."

"Of course," Akki said, "the scent glands dragged along the ground and the males would smell it and track a female down." She stopped. "But all those bones . . . dragons don't eat dragons. They're vegetarians. Only people eat dragons. And drakk."

"No one's been in these caves before. No one that I know of," Jakkin said. "Though old Likkarn said—"

And that was when the sending burst upon them full force.

It was a strange, wild, frenzied picture, a riot of grays shot through with angry, jagged blacks and icy silvers, reeking with fear. No common landscape, this one was tunnel-shaped and tunnel-twisted, but over and under and burrowing through was an unmistakable rainbow pattern, except that the only gradations of color were grays.

"That's Heart's Blood's pattern!" Jakkin screamed. "The rainbow. It's her. She's here!"

"Jakkin, no!" Akki cried, clawing at his arm. "She's dead. Heart's Blood is dead. No!" The walls returned her cry over and over.

But Jakkin was already running down the dark tunnel toward the sending.

Akki left the small safety of the wall and followed the sound of his pounding feet. Around a final bend she caught up to him and wrenched at the pack on his back, slowing him for a moment and slamming him against the wall. Just then something large and smelling of the familiar musk of dragon heaved past them, its dragging tail frantically whipping against the walls. The tail caught them both around the ankles and they fell heavily, Akki atop Jakkin's pack. She felt the jar of Boil break and the wetness spread beneath her. She whispered frantically, "That's not Heart's Blood, Jakkin. She's dead. We carved her open. Remember? We sheltered in her. Remember? I saw her bones."

His sobs began then, the racking sobs of someone unused to tears. At last he got hold of himself and sat up. "Sorry," he said, snuffling. "I know it's not her. But who—or what—is it?"

"I don't know," Akki said, putting her arms around him with a fierceness that astonished them both. "But I've got a feeling we're going to find out soon."

Akki took a deep breath, then urged Jakkin to do the same. In and out, in and out, they timed their respirations until they were both calm. And then they felt it, a great trembling presence nearby: breathy, hulking, and frightened.

"Man?" The dark sending was knife-sharp, though still within the basic tunnel shape, still gray. Then, tremulously, the sharper image melted away into a river of softer grays. *"Not man?"*

Jakkin stood and shed the soaking pack, then he walked slowly toward the creature with the sure step of a dragon trainer. All the while he thought cool and careful landscapes full of meadows and mountains, rivers and trees, gray-green, blue-gray. He put his hand out and rubbed down the dragon's enormous leg until the creature put its head to his hand and sniffed it carefully. It nudged his hand and he felt along the nose and over the bony ridge of the forehead till he came to its ears. He began to scratch around its earflaps.

Akki edged forward and tickled under the dragon's chin. She began to sing in a clear sweet voice:

> *Little flame mouths*
> *Cool your tongues,*
> *Dreaming starts soon*
> *Furnace lungs . . .*

And soon the tunnel was filled with a gentle thrumming and the dove-gray sendings of the cave dragon.

the
snatchlings

9

The dragon's thoughts were confusing. They seemed to hop from one splash of gray to the next. Its mouthings were un-formed as well, most of the time nothing more than the pipings of a new hatchling, as though it was not quite mute.

"Can you get any sense of her?" Akki asked.

"If you've found out *it* is a *her,* then you're doing better than I am," Jakkin said.

"I can *feel* the difference, idiot!"

"By her head?"

Akki sighed. "All this time with dragons and you don't know a worm-eaten thing. Female dragons have a special ridge under the tongue. You can just barely feel it when they're not gravid, but it's there. It grows bigger to help with the egg breaking if a hatchling's birth bump can't do the job. Then it gets smaller again, after the hatching."

"I got all of that but *gravid.*"

"It means pregnant, Jakkin. Full of eggs. *Honestly!* I some-times wonder about you."

Jakkin grunted. "You have a lot of head knowledge, Akki. But most of what I know comes from here." He tapped himself on the chest and his sending was a diagram of a human with the pulsing red point in the center of the body.

"That's the stomach, worm waste. Your heart is higher and on the left side." She laughed.

"I know that," Jakkin said quickly. But a moment later he joined in her laughter.

Sensing the lightened mood, the dragon gave a remarkable imitation of a chuckle, deep-throated and near a thrum. For an instant her mind seemed to clear and Jakkin caught a glimpse in her sending of a landscape so alien to him, he wondered if it was real. It was a dark hole in which hot fiery liquids bubbled, and nearly naked creatures, in stooped parody of human beings, bent over the boiling pit. Then the scene was gone, replaced by the same jumble of grays.

"Man? Not-man?" the dragon asked again.

"Of course man," Akki said.

The dragon leaped up, knocking Jakkin over with its tail as it stood and began to tremble.

"Oh, fewmets," Akki cried. "Jakkin, do something."

Jakkin scrambled to his feet and put both hands on the dragon's back. The only other time he had seen a dragon tremble that much had been in the Pit when a defeated dragon had screamed until Heart's Blood began to shake in the tremors known as Fool's Pride. Such trembling usually led a dragon to forget all training and fight to the death. But a death wish was not what Jakkin sensed from the cave dragon. He could read only total and overwhelming fear, so he willed himself to send calmly, though he could feel sweat running down his back with the effort. Forcing the image that had always worked for him before, he sent a faded, grayed-out picture of the oasis where he and Heart's Blood had trained, with its ribbon of blue river threading through the sandy landscape.

But the dragon seemed unable to listen. Her own hot, bubbling fear-images kept breaking into Jakkin's sending, boiling the gray-blue stream and turning the sand dunes into vast gray storms. Her trembling continued unabated.

"Man. Man. Man. Man." It was a kind of wail that ran through, around, under, and over the sending.

"I can't reach her, Jakkin shouted to Akki, his voice bouncing off the walls. "Either that or she can't hear."

"Maybe . . ." Akki's voice was thinned out, "maybe the pictures you're sending make no sense to her. Try something else." She'd begun trembling herself with the effort of soothing the dragon.

Jakkin moved toward the dragon's neck and put his arms around her shaking head. He blew into her ears, trying to get her attention.

"Listen, little flamemouth," he crooned, "I am no-man. I am part dragon. I had two mothers. Trust me. Trust me. Think of the dark. Think of the quiet. Think of the not-men." He forced cool, careful thoughts to her, stopping once to blow in her ears again, first the left, then the right. Then he started crooning again.

"I think . . ." Akki began, "I think she's trembling a little less."

He nodded, keeping up his croon. He babbled about caves and night and the moons and anything else that he could think of, but all the while he kept the sending as controlled as possible.

"She's *definitely* trembling less," Akki said.

Even Jakkin could feel it now, running his hand down the long neck where the scales, though shifting with small tremors, were moving more slowly. He doubled his effort then, sure of success. "I will tell you a story now," he said, his voice even, "about Fewmets Ferkkin, a fantastic fellow." He proceeded to tell the dragon seven jokes in a row without ever changing the tone of his voice. The important thing was to keep the words flowing.

Next to the dragon's leg, Akki relaxed into a giggle. "Jakkin— you're terrible," she said. But her mood, communicating directly with the dragon, helped even more.

As Jakkin began the eighth joke he realized he couldn't think of any more and finished lamely, "And that's all we know about Fewmets Ferkkin . . ." but it was all right, for the dragon had stopped shaking.

Jakkin sighed. "Now what is all this," he said softly, "about not-man?"

But the dragon, too, gave a tremendous sigh, lay down, and put her great head on her front legs and fell asleep.

"When you deal with hysterical babies," Akki said, "you'll find a surprising phenomenon—they fall asleep the minute the crisis is over."

"Some baby," Jakkin said.

"*Big* baby," Akki added.

They laughed, remembering their conversation only a day before.

"So now we have an enormous sleeping dragon on our hands," Jakkin began.

"And several enormous questions unanswered," Akki finished for him.

Jakkin was silent.

"One," Akki said, "is what is the difference between man and not-man and why did it scare her so much?"

"Two is—who is she and where did she come from?" Then, as if in afterthought, he added, "She's certainly too big to have come in through our entrance. And . . ."

"And if she came in elsewhere, where *is* elsewhere?" asked Akki.

"Three," Jakkin said, "who is she running from?"

"That's easy. The thing, whatever it is, that eats dragons and stacks their bones in neat piles." Akki gave an exaggerated shiver. It translated into wavy lines that streaked through Jakkin's head.

"Maybe. Maybe not," Jakkin said. "But that leads us right to question four, which is . . ."

"If man frightens her and not-man doesn't, then is it man who's doing all the eating?"

"*We* ate dragon meat before," Jakkin said.

They were both quiet for a moment, remembering.

"Maybe question five is—*what's down there?*" Akki said.

"Down where?" asked Jakkin.

"Question six," Akki said. "Which direction is *down there?*"

Jakkin squatted next to the sleeping dragon and put his back against the cave wall. "Question seven is—do we go forward or do we go back?"

Akki knelt next to him. "If we go back, we have to deal with the copter and whoever is in it."

Jakkin interrupted. "And the fact that there is no other way down the mountain."

She nodded. "But if we go forward, we have to deal with the dragon's fear and the man/not-man thing that eats dragons and licks the bones clean and whatever else in her sending we didn't understand."

"Hot bubbly somethings. And slope-shouldered creatures. And . . ."

"But that's all unknown," Akki said. "And maybe just in her imagination."

"Dragons don't have any imagination," Jakkin said. "They say only what is."

"But we *know* what's back there . . ."

"So the real question is?"

"Numbers eight, nine, and ten," said Akki. "Which is more frightening—what we know or what we don't know? The light world filled with copters and possible death or transportation, or the gray world filled with . . ." She stopped.

There was a long moment of silence. Jakkin tried to keep his mind blank, but it boiled with images. Finally he whispered to her, though his mind sent ahead what his mouth had formed reluctantly, "Both. They're both frightening. You choose. I'll do whatever you want."

"Hey," Akki whispered back, "that's *my* line!"

"Then we'll choose together."

"All right," Akki said. "We'll go . . ." Her mouth shut but her mind spiraled down and down and down into the unknown dark.

10

With their minds made up, Akki and Jakkin began to plan, and their voices crisscrossed the echoing cave.

"We need to wake up baby here," said Akki.

"I don't like calling her *baby here*," Jakkin said. "She should have a name."

"I thought I was the one who named things," Akki said, smiling. "You're always teasing me about it."

"Maybe I'm changing," Jakkin said.

"Maybe you're growing up," Akki retorted.

"Maybe you're not."

"Maybe the dragon already has a name," Akki said.

"Maybe you've changed the subject."

"Maybe she has."

"Akki, think. If a dragon has a name, it announces it in the first sending."

"How can she be this old and not have a name?" Akki asked.

"Question number eleven," Jakkin said.

"Well, she had a gray rainbow in her first sending. How about Rainbow Gray?"

"I hate it."

"Ssstep-sister."

"Don't be stupid."

"Then *you* name her," Akki said. "It was your idea, after all."

"All right, I will. What's the big vein that carries blood to the heart called again?"

"Anatomy lessons, Jakkin?"

"Yes. Sure. What's it called?"

"You mean the aorta?"

"*Aorta?* No, that's awful. You can't name a dragon Aorta."

"That's what it's called," Akki said.

"You told me something else."

"You mean . . ." Akki paused and added, "during one of my anatomy lessons?"

"Enough," Jakkin said. "I give up. So they weren't lessons, exactly. Only I did listen. You know a lot and I learned a lot."

Akki sighed. "You couldn't have learned much if you can't remember."

"Wait, I *do* remember. It's not the big vein, it's part of the heart. It's called . . ." He stopped, shrugging. "I can't remember."

"Right and left auricles?" asked Akki.

"That's it. Auricle. That's what I mean." There was excitement in his voice. "We'll call her Auricle, which sounds like *oracle*, which is a kind of omen."

"A good one, I hope," Akki said. "We could use some good luck."

"Auricle. I like that. Because she reminds me of Heart's Blood," Jakkin said. "Get it? Part of a heart is an auricle."

Akki put her hand out and touched Jakkin's arm. "She is no

relation to Heart's Blood, Jakkin. Don't keep hurting yourself that way."

"How do you know? Remember Blood's A Rover, one of the nursery dragons who went feral? He could have flown to these mountains. They're not far from the nursery. And if he did, and bred with other mountain dragons—well, Auricle and Heart's Blood *could* be related. Distant cousins. All of Sarkkhan's nursery dragons went back to a single breeding pair. So it's possible. No, even more than possible. It's probable. They're cousins."

Akki didn't answer, but her sending was dim and crackled around the edges.

"Anyway, we need to wake Auricle," Jakkin said.

As if on cue, the dragon began to grunt and snort, the usual sounds of a dragon rousing.

"Hello, Auricle," Jakkin said, stretching out the name itself and sending her a rainbow of grayish hearts.

The dragon ignored him and began grooming herself.

"Hey, worm waste, that's you!" Jakkin said. Then, switching to the more formal language of the dragon master, he added, "Auricle is thy name, little one." He punctuated it with a stronger sending.

The dragon looked up, its sending puzzled, fragmented. *"Name? No-name? Name? No-name?"*

"This one is either stupid, brain-damaged, or things are weirder down here than we imagined," Jakkin said.

Akki agreed, but put her hand on the dragon's neck and whispered into its ear, "Thy name is Auricle, little one. Auricle. For thou art part of Heart's Blood in that thou art part of something that belongs to the two of us, Jakkin and me."

At that the dragon's head snapped up, and in the not-quite-complete dark they could see the dark shrouds of her eyes.

"No-name," came the sending. *"Dragons no-name."* It bent its neck almost in two and waited, a gesture of such submission that Jakkin was shocked.

"Well, No-name," he said at last in exasperation, *"get yourself up. We are going to search for your bubbles and your man/no-man. Now. Up."* He said the last angrily and the sending was laced with a different kind of fire.

Akki added, "Go!"

The dragon leaped to its feet, its sending a mumble of grays and blacks. *"Up. Go. Man says. Man says. Man says. Up. Go."* It turned carefully around in the cave and with a slow, lumbering, shambling walk began to go back the way it had come.

Jakkin grabbed Akki's hand and squeezed it once. "Up and go, us, too," he whispered directly into her ear, so there was no echo.

As they walked down the spiraling tunnel, following the dragon, they expected things to become even darker, but instead the way seemed lighter. A fuzzy phosphorescence spattered the cave walls, spotty at first, and then in larger and larger patches. By the time they had gone around four or five deep bends, the tunnel was bathed in a gray-white glow that made the shadows they cast only darker.

Akki pulled on Jakkin's shirt and he turned, then gasped, for her face was gray and her mouth and eyes dark holes.

"You look strange," Akki said.

"You look like . . . a skull," Jakkin answered.

They didn't speak after that or look at each other, preferring to send little bits of comforting color back and forth between their bridged minds, reminders of the world outside, where gray was only a minor tint. But color was difficult to remember underground, and soon their sendings shaded off into the gray of the stone and shadow around them.

The walls grew damper to the touch, then progressively slimey. They could hear things dripping just out of sight. Twice Akki bumped into long fanglike pieces of rock that hung down from the ceiling, and once Jakkin tripped over a tooth of rock that protruded up from the floor. And still the tunnel spiraled down and down as they followed the large moving shadow that was the dragon's back and tail.

They heard a sudden loud splash and, turning a final bend, found themselves at the edge of a body of water.

Squinting his eyes, Jakkin realized that a small lake lay before them. He could just make out the dragon's head and neck protruding and throwing off ripples as it moved.

"Now what?" Jakkin asked.

Akki bent down and felt the water. "It's cold," she said.

"Well, we're part dragon," Jakkin said. "We should be able to stand the cold."

"The cold's not the problem," Akki said. "I . . . I can't swim."

Jakkin was silent for a moment, watching the dragon's head disappearing into the dark beyond.

"Maybe there's some other way around, some sort of ledge or path," Akki said.

"We don't have time," Jakkin said. "Auricle . . . the dragon . . . she's getting away."

"Then you swim after her, Jakkin, and I'll keep looking for another way and follow along after." Her voice was thin.

"I don't want to leave you," Jakkin said.

"Go!" Akki gave him a push.

He stumbled backward into the water, which was colder than

he'd expected, then he turned and splashed noisily after the dragon, his clothing slowing him down but not so much as to take him below. The sound of his swimming drowned out everything else. Once or twice he went under, but kept up his stroke. The water had a flat, metallic taste. When he opened his eyes under the water it was too dark to see anything. Blindly, he swam on.

The lake was not very large and he was on the other side quickly. But when he turned around the cave behind him was black. He couldn't see Akki at all.

"Akkkkkkkkkkki," he called out.

The sounds bounced crazily off the cave walls and it was some time before it was quiet again.

At last there came a tinny cry, neither plea nor call.

"Go on," said the voice. Or at least Jakkin thought that's what it sounded like. He mouthed the words back: "Go on."

He tried to send to her, but there was no response. All he received was a fuzzy static, a crackling that sputtered across his mind as if the water had somehow damaged his ability to receive. He shivered, more from fear than cold, then looked back over his shoulder to the passage where the dragon had disappeared.

"She said to go on," he urged himself. Then he hesitated for another long moment before he plunged into the passage after the worm.

11

Static still crackled through Jakkin's mind, blanking out even the lightest of sendings, but he could track the dragon by the trail of large puddles in the middle of three tunnels leading away from the lake. Jakkin searched his pockets frantically for a marker to leave for Akki. Finding none, he tore off a pocket instead and dropped it on the floor of the cave. It was the best he could do.

The middle tunnel curved downward at a steep slope, but it, too, was lit with patches of phosphorescence. They were at such regular intervals, Jakkin wondered if they had been placed there.

"Question number twelve," he thought grimly.

The tunnel took one last abrupt turning, and then, suddenly, he could see light ahead. It wasn't the bright white light of outdoors, but rather a flickering reddish glow. For a moment he wondered if he should wait for Akki to catch up to him. He turned and looked over his shoulder, straining into the darkness behind, but he couldn't see her. In fact, he couldn't see anything. For a moment he listened, but his crackle-filled mind reached nothing. The only way to go was forward, so he edged slowly toward the red light.

As he got closer he heard a kind of steady growl above the mind-crackling. It came from the same direction as the light. He moved forward again and began to distinguish two separate noises, one a low clanging and the other an echo. The closer he got, the more he became mesmerized by the light and sound. After so many hours in the cave, the color and noise both assaulted and drew him. Finally, overwhelmed by it all, he stopped, crouched down, and put his hands up over his ears. He squeezed his eyes tight until white sparks seemed to jump around in front of them.

For a long time he squatted, unmoving. Then slowly his mind cleared, as if he were waking up and knew he was waking, but wasn't yet shed of a dream. He opened his eyes, took his hands away from his ears, and stood. His knees gave a protesting creak.

The scene before him was as odd as anything he'd gotten from the dragon, as if it were a sending he couldn't read properly. He was on the far end of a large cavern lit by flames from a central pit that was as wide across as the Narakka River. Sitting on a grillwork over the flames were large pots filled with something that glowed now red and now shadow. Above the pots, on an overhang of rock, were half a dozen leaning figures stirring the pots with long sticks.

Were they men or not-men? Auricle's puzzlement became his own. Men and not-men. These creatures had a man's form, muscular and stockier than anyone Jakkin had ever known. But there was something really wrong with the shape. They were much too broad in the shoulder, much too short in the leg. Men and not-men.

One of the creatures saw Jakkin, pointed at him, and without a sound they all looked up.

Jakkin felt his head suddenly filled with strings of picture-questions. Like the sending of dragons, the questions were wordless and yet completely understandable.

"Who you?" The thoughts came in sharp stabs of light. *"You? You? Who you?"* It was not one mind but a number of them asking the question. He could feel the differences as clearly as if they'd been individual voices.

Jakkin shouted at them across the pit, not yet trusting his mind, needing to feel the precision of words in his mouth. Akki was right about that. "I am Jakkin. Jakkin Stewart. From Sarkkhan's Nursery. Bondsman and trainer. Master now." He felt no need to disguise who he was. Surely these creatures knew nothing about the Rokk Pit. Unaccountably, his hand went to his chest, his fingers fumbling for the bondbag that had hung there for so many years. Then he gave a short, staccato laugh. None of that seemed to mean *anything* to them. He'd try another tack. "I am Jakkin Stewart of the mountains. Out of Heart's Blood. Who are you?"

That seemed to reach them. They put down their sticks and looked at one another, gesturing wildly but still not speaking aloud. Then, as if on a signal, they all turned and faced him, staring. Their eyes, even from so far away, seemed to glow like an animal's in the dark.

Jakkin felt his mind fill up again until he felt it would overflow, for the sending was so loud and overpowering, he couldn't move. It was like Akki's first sendings multiplied a hundredfold. Hot points of sizzling lights danced in his brain.

How long he stood there, stupefied, he couldn't have said, but suddenly he felt a painful slap on his cheek and he could see and move again, his mind cleared. In front of him stood the man who had delivered the blow, arm still upraised. A man. Definitely. Stocky, broad-shouldered, hulking, but unquestionably a man. He was stripped down to a skin loin cloth, his feet in leather sandals, his chest hairy, his head smooth. But a man.

Despite the stinging cheek, Jakkin smiled at him. The man was a full head shorter than he was.

"I told you who I was," Jakkin said. "Who are you?"

The man raised his hand again. This time Jakkin saw the blow as well as felt it, yet he couldn't move from it or respond in kind, for at the same time a ringing admonition leaped into his mind.

"Do not krriah, youngling. You not child. Still you give child's krriah. Be man."

Bewildered, Jakkin felt himself cast loose of this second mind-spell. He put his hand to his cheek. He could still feel the heat of the blow beneath his fingers.

"I Makk." The sending was short, brutal, final. But whether that was his name, his title, or some other designation was not clear.

Before Jakkin could respond, Makk grabbed his arm and jerked him forward until his feet were curled over the lip of the rock. For a moment Jakkin was afraid Makk meant to push him over into the flames. For a short man, he was very powerful. As another protest started to form on his lips, Jakkin felt instructions insinuate themselves in his head. He glanced down at his feet. Below, where his toes curled over the rim, was a rough-carved set of steps.

"Down!"

He had no choice. With Makk at his back, Jakkin carefully made his way down the stone steps, hugging the rock face as he went. He could hear the whisper of the man's feet behind him as he descended, and his head seemed filled with an alien presence he couldn't quite shake loose. The only thing he could do—and he did it with deliberate care—was to keep Akki's face out of his thoughts. She must not be caught, as he was, by the not-man men.

12

The steps followed the curve of the cave wall and came out on the far side of the pit. Jakkin could feel the heat on his right side and he longed to turn and say something to the man behind him, but the slap and the strange word *kkriah* were burned into his memory. Until he knew more he would not chance speaking aloud again.

Their steps echoed in the vast chamber, and Jakkin stopped for a moment, unsure which way he should proceed. He felt Makk's rough hand on his shoulder turning him toward the left, where there was another tunnel. Once they entered it he was cool again, and he welcomed the dark and the relative quiet.

Makk shoved him along the tunnel and Jakkin went slowly, trying to shutter his mind against the barrage of questions/instructions. The minute he closed the imagined door he felt a kind of release of pressure, as if the man had simultaneously stopped searching around in his thoughts. The oddness of it made him raise his eyebrows, but he kept moving.

The tunnel ended abruptly in another large cavern, but this one was not lit with fires. Instead there was a complete wall of phosphorescence that made the cave a place of deep shadows. Over thirty men were in the room, some sitting at long tables eating, some sleeping on rocky outcroppings, some apparently in deep conversations, for their hands moved as if shaping images, though their mouths were still. It reminded Jakkin of an evening in the nursery bondhouse, though it was certainly much quieter. And the memory ached like a rotten tooth when he probed it further.

"What is . . ." Jakkin began aloud, and was stunned into silence by the violence of a multiple sending. He began again, this time only with his mind. *"What is this place?"*

Makk put a hand on his shoulder again. *"This Place of Men."* The pictures he sent were straightforward and without any of the subtleties or undertones Jakkin associated with Akki's sendings.

"What about . . . women?"

"Place of Women not here. There." The image Makk sent was of a different cavern in which stocky, broad-shouldered women with long, straight dark hair ate, sat, slept in poses similar to those of the men. It was not a symbol of a place but the place itself, as sharply delineated as a picture.

Makk's sending continued. *"There, too, Place of Those Who Kkriah. There, too, Place of Great Mothers."* The last image he sent was that of dragons huddled together as if they were clutchmates, though they ranged in shape and age.

"Dragons?" Jakkin sent, and when there was no answer he added, *"Worms?"* Each image was slightly different.

Makk shook his head. He sent a gray picture of dragons hovering over a pile of eggs. The meaning was clear. *"Great Mothers."* It was reinforced by all the men.

Jakkin rubbed his head behind the right ear, where an ache

was starting. A bad one, he guessed, and nothing to laugh at to help it bleed away. He drew a deep breath, ready to begin again. Sending this way was hard work, like speaking a strange language. Just then his stomach rumbled and all the men laughed. Their laughter was silent, a bubbly mind-sending that made him almost giddy.

"You hunger," Makk sent. *"You eat."*

"I'd love to eat," Jakkin sent back, his images laced with an ironic edge that spoke of other kinds of hunger: sleep, the need to understand, and a very dim image of Akki, which leaked out unbidden and which he quickly suppressed. But Makk seemed oblivious to anything but the central message.

"You eat," he sent again, signaling one of the sitters with those curious finger-waggles. The man stood and brought over a bowl for Jakkin.

Jakkin sniffed at the bowl. It smelled like dragon stew. Hungry as he was, Jakkin's stomach revolted. *"Dragon?"* he queried. Then, remembering, he added, *"Great Mother?"*

The sending that came back to him, so solid and unemotional, chilled him. *"What else?"*

He put the bowl on the nearest table and shook his head. *"No!"*

"You insult Great Mother's gift?" Even the sleepers stirred at that sending.

"I'm not that hungry. I can't eat." How could he explain to these crude cave dwellers that once he'd made full contact with dragons, eating their meat was impossible. His stomach chose that moment to growl again.

The bubbling response of the men was far out of proportion to the joke, and Jakkin suddenly wondered if any involuntary body noise was funny to these silent men. He tried to explain his refusal to eat meat as clearly and directly as he could. *"My . . . people . . . do not eat Great Mothers."* It was not exactly a lie. He and Akki were a separate people now.

"Ancestors warn of such people." Makk's sending seemed tinged with an emotion other than anger for the first time.

"Your ancestors. Tell me." Maybe, Jakkin hoped, careful to keep the thought hidden, maybe here was a real clue, a way out of this place.

Makk's face softened, as if the question somehow pleased him. His sending began and it had the rhythms of a story long rehearsed and often told. *"First were The Men. Strong Men. Men of Bonds."* He held up his wrists, and for the first time Jakkin noticed he wore metal bracelets.

Metal! Jakkin gasped aloud. There was so little metal on Austar that what there was had to be carefully husbanded for use in the cities. The cost of metal was far beyond the ordinary bonder. Even most masters could afford little. He remembered the grillwork under the great pots in the fire cavern. And the pots themselves. And the sticks! They were all metal. How could he have been so blind. These strange men had a secret the outside world would love to have—a secret metal cache. If he listened carefully, perhaps he could find out more.

Makk was continuing. *"One man, First Makker, knew to take Stone. Knew to turn Stone to Ore. From Ore comes The Fire That Is Water. From The Fire That Is Water come Bands. For we were of Bonds who now are of Bands."*

There was a poetry in Makk's sending that almost obscured the story he told. Drawing a curtain between Makk's mind and his own, Jakkin tried to find the real meaning. Could First Makker have been an escaped prisoner back in the days of all their grandfathers? Someone with a working knowledge of metal-making who had somehow managed to live through the deadly cold. Jakkin knew that not all the early prisoners were murderers and thieves. A few had been political prisoners sent away from Earth or other planets to the metal-poor desert world of Austar. Some of those prisoners must have had skills beyond the ordinary. What if that First Makker was one? And what if other escapees had joined him and remained hidden within the bowels of the mountains, generation after generation? It made sense. Makk said they were Men of Bonds. And if the secret of the metal-making had passed down from father to son over the years . . . He suddenly realized Makk had stopped sending and was staring at him. Jakkin stared back, the wall around his thoughts carefully constructed again.

Makk nodded and the sendings came again. *"We Men of Great Mother. Flesh of her flesh. Blood of her blood. One day go to place of Bonds and throw them over."* The sending was dark red, the red of anger and fire and blood, but Makk's hands were raised as if in ecstasy.

Jakkin didn't understand what that meant at all. Some ritual of eating, perhaps? What if they insisted he eat with them? Could he do it? Did he dare refuse again? And if these strange men really did plan to go outside and fight, shouldn't he warn the outsiders? After all, the closest civilized place to these mountains was Sarkkhan's Nursery, where he had grown up. His friends were there. But if he managed to get out, the last place he should go would be the nursery. Surely any searchers would have spies there.

His mind in a turmoil, he drew in a breath and carefully drew aside the curtain over his thoughts to let a sending out. *"The Great Mothers, where are they? And where is the Place of Women?"*

Makk lowered his hands and came close to Jakkin, touching him on the shoulder. *"What place you? Too high for here. Too thin for here. No Bands. Yet speak without noise. Not like Others."*

"Others? What others?"

"Long ago Others." He did not elaborate.

A man who had been sitting at the far end of the table stood up and came over to Jakkin, placing his hand on top of Makk's. *"What place?"*

Jakkin thought a long time before answering, careful to cloak his mind till the last. Sweat beaded his forehead. *"I come from another Place, another mountain, another cave."* He knew suddenly that to admit being from the outside was inviting death. *"There we wear no Bands but we, too, know the Great Mothers. I am blood of the blood with a great red."* He wouldn't tell them *how* he'd shared the dragon's blood, though her rainbow sign broke across his sending, a memory of that generous spirit he couldn't keep out.

The colorful sending seemed to startle the men. Makk's hand dropped from his shoulder and everyone drew away mentally. Jakkin wondered if it was the color or the joy in the sending that had so provoked them. Then he shook his head, continuing:

"I came to your place with my . . . woman." He bet Akki would be furious if she knew he'd called her that.

Makk nodded, but still kept his distance. *"Yes. We know this. She in Place of Women."*

It was Jakkin's turn to be startled. He walked over to Makk and put his hand on the man's broad shoulder. At the touch he was able to see right into Makk's mind. So that was it! He made the sending as strong as he could: *"I want my woman. That is how it is done in my place."* When he took his hand away Makk's mind snapped shut like some kind of trap.

Makk's fingers moved swiftly, then his sharp sending pierced Jakkin's mind. *"Now you eat."*

"Not that stuff."

Turning, Makk signed toward one of the men at a table. He rose and brought over another bowl. This one was filled with a dark jellied substance. Jakkin took the bowl and tipped it eagerly into his mouth. He recognized congealed Boil and chikkberries, but there was also a greenish, bittersweet taste that lingered after he had finished the food and made his mouth feel clean and good.

Only later did he realize what that meant: chikkberries and Boil. The men of the cave didn't just stay inside. Somewhere there had to be an easy access to outside, to a meadow. He wondered when and how he dared to ask.

13

Makk made it clear, though it took many sendings, that if Jakkin didn't work like the other men, he wouldn't be fed again. Nor would he be allowed to go to the Place of Women when it was time.

"Time?" Jakkin had sent, hoping for an explanation. He'd already given up on the food. Somehow, somewhere, there was a supply of fresh growing things, but certainly not in the bowels of the cave.

But Makk had only reiterated the same images, of sun and moons, clear notations of time. And since there was no way for Jakkin to find the Place of Women on his own, or to feed himself, for that matter, he worked. He wasn't happy about it, but he worked, reminding himself to stay alert and learn as much as he could.

Standing on the high shelf of rock and taking his turn at stirring pots of fire, Jakkin felt alternately hot and cold. The flames seared his front, but there was a cold breeze across his shoulders and along the backs of his knees. His arms ached from the unaccustomed labor and his mind was weary from the twin efforts of cloaking and listening. But the more he saw of the metal-making operation, the more he realized its importance. And the more he realized bitterly that he was powerless to let the rest of Austar know.

After hours with the great iron rod, Jakkin was relieved by a silent, hulking worker who signaled him with a hand on the back. When Jakkin turned away from the shelf there was Makk again, ready to lead him to another portion of the cave where men were grubbing around the walls, using metal picks the size of fewmet shovels, mining out the stuff Makk called Ore. Following behind these men was a crew of workers with sling bags full of phosphorescent moss, which they placed wherever a vein of the Ore had been picked out. Despite Makk's attempts at explanation, and the instruction of his own eyes and ears, Jakkin wasn't sure if the moss was used as tunnel markers for the pickers, for light, for decoration, or a combination of all three.

By the time it was his turn on the moss detail, Jakkin was openly yawning, but no one seemed to notice. The bag's straps were made for broader shoulders than his and kept slipping. The cool, flaky mosses were not as easy to set in place as he'd thought. They had to be bent and shaped and tucked into the ore holes, and most of the time they crumbled between his inept fingers.

He was just beginning to get the feel of it, under the gruff tutelage of a one-eyed man he called Brekk (his sign was simply a single staring eye) when there was a loud gonging that echoed and re-echoed off the cave walls. At the sound, so loud in the enforced silence of the tunnels, the men set down their tools and bags and shuffled to the main cavern. Jakkin followed them.

It was only when he was back in the main cave that he realized it was a shift change, much like Sarkkhan's Nursery, where a few of the bondboys had night-watch duty and others worked in the day. He almost laughed aloud remembering his friends Errik-kin, who loved being in bond, and Slakk, who'd try anything to get out of work.

Brekk pushed him toward a small crevice where there was a grassy pallet set upon the stone. He gave Jakkin a brief smile that shut his one good eye and left the empty socket staring.

"Sleep!" he commanded, the picture being one of a face with both eyes closed. It was accompanied by a kind of mental hum-song.

Jakkin needed no further urging. He climbed into his sleep crevice and lay down on the grass. He was just wondering that it was so fresh and sweet-smelling when sleep overcame him, and with it strange dark dreams.

That same pattern of work and sleep, broken by silent meals, continued for a number of rotations. Jakkin lost all real sense of time in the half-light of the caves. He had no idea whether he worked for hours or days at a time, but simply slogged along until the gong. After a while he almost forgot there *was* anything but the caves, holding only to Makk's promise that they would even-tually go to the Place of Women, where Akki was being kept.

As he found himself slipping into the same kind of somnam-bulant shuffle as the others, he tried to rouse himself with spoken speech. He worked as far from the men as he could manage, whispering little ditties in a voice that carried no farther than his own shadow. He knew if he didn't talk to himself, he would eventually lose the use of ear and tongue. So he recited Fewmets Ferkkin stories, hummed old ballads, even found he'd a gift for verse. He made up seventeen different stanzas of a poem that began "There once was a bondboy named Jakkin . . ." using *lackin', snackin',* and *trackin'* among the rhymes. When he really became bored with his own company and felt himself slipping back into the half-sleep, he invented imaginary dialogues with Akki. She ended every one of these conversations with a hug. He got so he could feel her arms around him, the softness of her cheek on his.

One time he tried to slip away down an empty passage, but Makk caught him before he was around the first turn, and cuffed him soundly. Jakkin returned to the others, his ears ringing and his mind filled with the angry mutterings of the other men. But he noticed he wasn't the only one cuffed. Brekk had his head knocked a few times, and another man, Orkkon, was roughed up for dropping his iron stirring stick. But Orkkon was ill, not lazy, and after a second beating he lay on his pallet three rotations, tossing and sweating. He never moaned aloud, though his send-ings were filled with formless dark clouds that Jakkin read as fever.

It was a wonder to Jakkin that the work was such an endless drudgery and that the men bore it without complaining. What they did was not any more difficult or arduous than the tasks he'd done at Sarkkhan's Nursery, but there was no variety. And there were no voices. He decided that it was the human voice he missed the most—that and the brightly colored sendings of the dragons. Sound and light. Without those, how could a person survive?

And yet—his traitor mind continued—these men of the mountains survived, and thrived. Men—and not-men. Survived but at a price. Jakkin guarded his thoughts as he made a list of the things these cavemen lacked: warmth, emotion, laughter, love—all those things that made life worthwhile. The list com-forted him.

"I *will* get out of here," he whispered to himself. "I'll find Akki and go. Anything on the outside will be bearable after this boredom. Anything." And then he remembered Heart's Blood dying, shook his head, and was silent.

It was the ninth or tenth rotation—he'd lost count somewhere along the way—when a runner came to the men as they ate. Jakkin knew him for a stranger even from far away because he was younger than the rest and dressed differently. He was wearing a kind of light-colored woven cloth instead of the loin cloths of the Ore workers or the darker coveralls of the miners, which were made of the eggskin that hatchlings shed.

The boy's sending was frantic, emotional, full of color, which further marked him.

"Great Mother trembles," he sent, a maelstrom of dark tones. *"She pants. Her birth hole swells. It does not open. All our women fear."*

Makk and the other men made a tight circle around the boy. Putting his hand on the boy's shoulder, Makk sent, *"I come. Orkkon comes, whose father's father was First Healer."*

The circle broke apart and reformed around Orkkon, who still lay sweating on his pallet. Jakkin, on the far edges of the circle, watched as Makk knelt by Orkkon and put a hand on his head.

"You come," Makk sent.

Orkkon managed, with Makk's support, to sit up. Jakkin could see the sweat running down his chest and the flush on his cheeks. He seemed to be having trouble breathing.

"You come with me," Makk sent again.

There was no answering pattern from Orkkon. His mind seemed as flushed and sweaty as his body.

"Wait!" Jakkin cried aloud, wincing as the men turned toward

him with another brutal, dark sending. At least he had gotten
their attention. *"Wait,"* he sent. *"I am a Dragon Healer in my
own place. Let Orkkon stay here. He is too sick anyway. Let me
go instead."*

Makk pushed the sweating man back down on his bed and
stood. As he walked toward Jakkin, Jakkin put out his hand.
Puzzled, Makk stopped for a moment, then moved forward
again. He took Jakkin's hand in his. The instant they touched
Jakkin could feel his mind being invaded and he willed it to show
pictures of himself and Heart's Blood in the cavernous incubarn.
His memory flooded back and he took the memory, shaping it to
his own use. There was the dark barn and the great hen towering
over him, the fire in her eyes now warm and inviting. Then the
great red circling the room in the peculiar halting rhythm of the
pregnant female. Next he showed her squatting over the shallow
hole dug into the sandy floor. All the while Jakkin soothed her.
"Easy, easy, my beauty, easy, easy, my red." He moved the sending forward, concentrating on the nest itself as the eggs cascaded
from the dragon's birth channel into the hole. *"This I have done
many times,"* his sending promised. He masked his traitorous
afterthought that *many* was a gross exaggeration.

For a moment Makk didn't respond, though there seemed to
be a murmured sending from the other men, approval of some
sort. At last Makk sent a black ropelike form shooting into Jakkin's sending, whipping around the arm of the boy pictured
there and dragging the dreamboy away. Like all of Makk's sendings, it was unambiguous in its meaning.

"Come," said his sending. *"Great Mother needs. Come."*

14

The three of them trotted down the tunnels, and though Jakkin tried to mark the way, they made too many turnings and switchbacks for him to remember. Yet, fast as they traveled, Makk and the boy never hesitated; the tunnels seemed to be as familiar to them as the hallways in a nursery bondhouse.

Jakkin wondered what he would find when they reached the Place of Great Mothers. Would the dragon giving birth be Auricle? He doubted that. She hadn't been obviously pregnant and, in fact, had dragged her tail like a dragon in heat. Besides, it took four months for eggs to develop, so there couldn't have been time. But a little fear nagged at him. What did he really know about time inside the caves? It felt like a week or two, but without access to the sun and moons, he couldn't tell day from night, much less the passage of a week.

Besides, these men were so different—thicker, heftier, duller, speechless—perhaps dragons in the mountains were different as well. Certainly Auricle had seemed odd, almost brain-damaged, or like an infant unused to either light or sound. Now that he'd met and worked with the men of the cave, he understood the dragon better.

Makk and the boy stopped suddenly and Jakkin caught up with them. They had paused just inside the entrance to another large cavern. It seemed lighter and airier than the tunnels, and Jakkin squinted, looking around. High above them was a small opening and, far above that, a wan light like a pale lantern. He stared at it for several moments before he realized it was one of the moons. So—they *could* see outside; they *did* have a way to measure time. He laughed out loud and was cuffed by Makk for the sound.

Clenching his fists, Jakkin turned on Makk, but the man was already walking away, through another arched doorway. That it was a doorway and not just the beginning of a tunnel became clearer to Jakkin the closer he came to it. The stone on both sides of the arch had been intricately carved with figures of dragons: dragons fighting, dragons flying, dragons mating, dragons giving birth. They were illuminated by torches set on either side of the doorway.

Jakkin raced through the doorway after Makk and the boy and gasped in surprise. Unlike the rough, unadorned caves where the men lived, in this well-lit cavern was a series of stalls chiseled into the stone. In places the stone itself was fluted like curtains, in others there were detailed carvings of men, women, and dragons all entwined.

In the stalls to the left close to twenty dragons were roped, their shadows moving sluggishly against the walls. Silent gray-brown presences, they sent only beige images into Jakkin's mind, so different from the usual raucous colors that challenged him whenever he'd entered the nursery barns. The beige sendings were pale questions that floated slowly across his mind before drifting away, like clouds across a sky.

Jakkin looked carefully at the dragons in their stalls and sent back his own questions, trying to locate Auricle. But if she was there, he wasn't able to identify her.

"This is the Place of the Great Mothers?" Jakkin queried, puzzled because none of the stalled dragons looked old enough to be mated.

"Place of Little Mothers," Makk sent back. *"We go farther."* He motioned with his head and walked on.

They went through another arched door, this one decorated with a pattern of egg-shaped bulges.

"Who did all this?" Jakkin's mind buzzed with the question. He hadn't meant to send it, but his curiosity couldn't be contained.

"The Makker made this." Makk stepped through the archway. The boy remained behind, but Jakkin went after Makk.

If the outer cavern had been a surprise, this room was an astonishment. It held only three stalls, but each was as spacious as a room in the nursery incubarn. The first stall was occupied by a greenish-gray dragon a little smaller than Sssasha, placidly munching on something Jakkin didn't immediately recognize. The second stall contained a pale red dragon who seemed to be sleeping. Both dragons were pregnant, their stomachs bulging, their tails flattened and drooping on the floor.

He heard a panting noise in the third and largest stall. Jakkin peered in. Two broad-shouldered women were kneeling over a large brown dragon. The dragon was lying on her side and breathing noisily, tongue lapping the side of her mouth and her earflaps trembling.

"The Great Mother fails." Makk looked over Jakkin's shoulder; his brief judgment brutally apt.

The women looked up simultaneously. Although as thickly built as Makk, their faces as blunt and unattractive, they had more emotion in their expressions. The older one pushed her lank dark hair away from her eyes; the younger one sighed. One of them sent a tired gray thought: *"Yes. She fails."*

Jakkin went into the stall and moved around the women. He knelt by the dragon's head and touched one earflap. The skin vibrated against his hand in a fast, erratic manner. Not a good sign. He pried open one of the dragon's eyes with his fingers, being extremely careful not to tear the inner membrane. A dulled eye stared back at him but did not respond to the torchlight. Another bad sign. He noticed the tongue. A healthy dragon's tongue was rough and ridged. This one was smooth and velvety, and that meant fever for sure. A very high fever.

He stood, stepped over the dragon's neck, and walked beside the spine toward the tail.

Gesturing downward, he sent an order to the women: *"Hold the tail away from the Great Mother's body."*

The younger woman stood and came over to the tail. She picked it up, exposing the birth canal.

Jakkin ducked under and examined the channel. It was clogged with pulpy masses, angry swellings the color of a bruise. When he touched one with a tentative finger, the dragon moaned out loud, a sound so foreign in the cave, it echoed eerily. The woman dropped the tail.

Jakkin stood and turned to Makk. He knew he might not get another opportunity and so he formed his sending with great care. *"My woman. The one you found. She is a healer. She makes sick ones well. If we are together, she and I, we can save this*

Great Mother." He made the sending as positive as he could, though under his breath he murmured, "I hope."

Makk was concentrating too hard on his sending to notice.

When Makk gave no answer Jakkin sent again; this time his image was unambiguous and linear. He pictured Akki as tall and clean, bright-eyed, narrow-shouldered, and beautiful. Very beautiful.

"*No!*" Makk sent suddenly, his sending knifing across Jakkin's. "*This one*"—and his picture was of a girl thin, malformed, ugly —"*this one can bear. Only women past bearing serve Great Mothers.*"

Jakkin thought a minute. He would have to lie. He wondered whether these people understood lying. It must be very hard to lie if all you had were the thoughts in your head. Lying was much easier with words. He drew in a deep breath and began, "*My woman is a healer and in my Place healers do not bear children.*"

Makk's eyes grew wider and he gave what might be mistaken for a smile. "*Good!*"

"*When?*" Jakkin's sending was as clipped as Makk's, a single sharp stab of light.

"*Soon.*"

"*If it is not soon,*" Jakkin sent, kneeling again by the dragon and slipping his hand under the dragon's tail, "*this Great Mother will die and her eggs will crack open inside her.*" He touched one of the pulpy masses again, put his hand around it, and quite deliberately squeezed.

The dragon screamed.

Makk and the two women placed their hands over their ears and the younger woman fell to her knees. But Jakkin, even though he hated bringing pain to the beast, nonetheless reveled in the sound.

15

By the time the echo of the scream had faded, Jakkin was once again at the dragon's head, checking its eyes and tongue. There was no change. He put his head down by the dragon's mouth and breathed deeply. The smell was slightly sour, not unusual for a dragon, but also strangely bland. In the nursery such a smell usually meant a worm needed extra rations of burnwort, but he'd no idea what they fed dragons here.

At the head of the stall was an iron hook on which several handfuls of dry grasses hung. Jakkin walked over and tore out some. Crumbling it between his fingers, he spread it along his palm. He could identify sedgeseeds and skkagg grass, but there were other things new to him, including a fleshy wine-colored fungus. In the nursery they'd never feed a dragon that. What was it Likkarn used to say? *Mushrooms red, dragon dead.* He held out his hand and pointed to it. *"This?"* he sent bluntly.

The older woman came over to him and stared at his hand. She didn't meet his eyes, and her sending was so tentative, he couldn't make out any name for the fungus. But it was obviously no surprise to her.

Still, he asked again because of Likkarn's warning and because food was always the first thing examined when a dragon fell sick. It was just too easy to poison one of them, large as they were, especially a fighting dragon at one of the major Pits. He held out his hand and this time sent directly to the woman before him, *"This?"*

The woman's answer was clearer this time, though she still wouldn't look up at him. *"That makes bearing easy. Women eat too."*

Jakkin nodded and let the stuff drift to the floor. Both women were quick to broom it away, which made Jakkin smile. No wonder these stalls were so clean. No fewmets, no extra straw, no pieces of half-chewed meals. The women were quicker at their tasks than any stallboy he'd ever known, including himself. He turned back to the dragon. Her tail was twitching ever so slightly.

"Lift that tail again!"

This time both women hauled the tail up and to the side.

Jakkin knelt down. A grayish fluid was leaking from the birth channel. He put his hand in and discovered that the swelling he'd squeezed had burst. The smell of it was overpowering.

Hearing a noise behind him, he turned around. Akki was standing at the entrance to the stall.

"Akk—" he started to say aloud, and her hand went immediately up as if to cover his mouth.

"Shhh," came her sending, a bright green cloud covering the mouth of a golden sun. It was the loveliest color he'd seen in ages. *"Later."* She smiled.

It was only after Akki knelt to examine the dragon that Jakkin realized she'd lost weight and her hair was dirty and tangled.

There was a bruise under her right eye and a scratch along her right arm. He wanted both to hold her and to shout at her and shake her. But when she turned around at his bubbling sending, he suddenly remembered he'd told Makk she was a healer and not to be thought of as a woman-who-bears. He had to treat her with the cold deference due such a one as long as Makk's people could overhear their sendings.

"I'm glad you have come, My Healer. I have told Makk and his men of your many skills."

Akki understood at once and nodded at him, gesturing that he kneel by her side.

He kept a careful distance between them, sketching in what he knew of the dragon's condition. It was hard to do in a sending. Akki was right about words. But as he formed the pictures Akki followed along, performing the same tests he'd just done. The dragons earflaps still vibrated erratically, and the eyes remained fixed. But the tail had a tiny touch of resilience now.

When she finished her palpation of the birth channel, Akki turned and looked directly at him. *"You're right. The channel is clogged and we'll have to lance those boils.* She wrinkled her nose. *"But without the proper tools . . . I can't guarantee a worse infection won't set in."*

The women didn't stir as her complex sending filled their minds. If they understood it, they gave no sign. Makk shuffled self-consciously. But Jakkin just grinned. Her sending had been filled with wonderful asides, bright-colored pictures that told him more in a single sending then all the dull patterns the mountain clan had offered the whole time he'd been there. But her sending had hidden messages as well: oblique warnings of other dangers, plus a joyous rainbow under which a green tree was twined with a bright blue vine. He knew Makk would never guess what those private images meant. Akki was saying she loved him.

Akki stood, brushed her hair back over her ears, and looked straight at Makk. He seemed uneasy with her direct gaze, shifting his eyes right and left.

"Bring me water," Akki said. *"Boil it. Bring me knives but first put them in the fire. Bring me cloth. It must be clean."* Then, as an afterthought, really more a mental sigh, she added, *"What I'd give for my pack. It had my medkit in it."* The picture of the kit lying on the cave floor was skillfully rendered.

Makk's eyes seemed to shutter for a moment, and then, as if making up his mind, nodded to a man standing in the doorway and broke into rapid hand signs. The man nodded back and took off down a tunnel to the right of the stalls.

Jakkin watched him go, his curiosity uncurtained. He was still staring after the man when he felt a hand on his arm. Turning, he saw it was Akki. She pulled him close, whispering so quietly he had to strain to hear it, "I think they know where the pack is, Jakkin. It's got your knife in it, the one Golden gave to you."

He didn't dare answer her, not even with a sending.

The man returned in minutes with the unopened pack. He handed it carefully to Akki, as if he were afraid of her, making sure their hands did not touch. She took it coldly, then knelt again by the dragon's tail.

At the same time the two women came back with an iron pot filled with steaming water, the younger woman also carrying two fairly crude knives and strips of yellow weaving.

Rooting around in her pack, Akki found the silver knife. She plunged it into the pot of water and held it there, as if ticking off seconds. Jakkin could feel her visualization of a clock and wondered if the others knew what it was. At the count of sixty she withdrew the knife and held it up to the torchlight, examining it.

"If you know any prayers . . ."

To Jakkin's surprise, the women began a sending that was a repetition of patterns, like a chant. It had an intensity beyond anything they'd sent before. He knew it had to be a prayer.

Akki gestured for him to kneel beside her and he scrambled to do her bidding.

"Now!" she sent.

He held the dragon's tail away while she slid the knife into the birth channel and punctured the first of the bruise-colored boils.

Jakkin had never participated in an operation before, though he'd had some experience with minor doctoring in the nursery. One of the nursery stud dragons, Blood Sucker, had frequent mouth infections that always needed attention. And he'd watched countless wingtips sewn up after fights. But this was different and he marveled at how calm Akki remained.

He knew enough to soak the woven strips in the hot water. Then, holding the tail away with his left hand, he wrung out the strips with his right, using the cloth to soak up any infection. When he withdrew the rag and dropped it onto the floor, the waiting women whisked it away. Over and over they repeated their tasks until the work assumed its own rhythms, which coincided with the dragon's labored breathing.

All of a sudden Akki withdrew her arm from the channel, sat back on her heels, and sighed out loud. She was soaked with sweat. The bruise under her eye seemed to reflect the yellow of the light and the infection. Jakkin guessed he looked as bad, but he smiled at her.

Wiping a filthy hand across her forehead, Akki stood and looked at Makk, focusing a sending on him. *"The Great Mother will live. The women must keep cleaning her. In a day or two she should be healed. Then the eggs will drop.*"

Makk nodded. "*Good.*"

"Damned right!" Akki said aloud.

Automatically Makk raised his hand, but Akki stared him down and slowly his hand lowered. It happened so fast, Jakkin hadn't had time to stand, but as Makk's hand went down Jakkin got to his feet. He touched Akki's shoulder.

Akki sent, "*We need to wash. We are covered with sickness. Take us to a place of water.*"

Jakkin added, "*Place of much water. Like a lake.*"

Makk made a face and looked uneasy. Then he nodded curtly and signed to the two men in the doorway. Squaring his shoulders, he turned and left.

The men led them through a wide, unadorned tunnel whose turnings were sparingly lighted by widely spaced phosphorescent mosses. After only half a dozen bends they found themselves at the edge of a small lake.

For a long moment Akki hesitated, and Jakkin remembered that she couldn't swim. He reached out for her hand and led her, fully clothed, into the cold dark water. When they were waist deep he let go and let himself sink down to the lake bottom, thankful for the touch of the clean water on his face and through his hair. When he surfaced Akki was standing where he'd left her, staring out into the darkness. He tried to reach her mind to assure her and was rewarded instead with a crackling sound. He realized that once again his mind had been closed by the water to any sendings.

Motioning with his hand, he tried to call her toward him but she didn't move, only stared at him strangely. So he went over and led her into even deeper water, away from the two men who glowered at them from the rock ledge.

"I can't hear any sendings now," he whispered. "The water blocks it. You go under, too, Akki."

She turned her back on the men and whispered back, "I wondered why you didn't answer me."

"Put your head under and you'll see."

Dipping her hands in the water, as if she were still washing, Akki hesitated. "I can't," she whispered.

"Can't what?"

"Can't put my head under."

"Why not?"

"I'm too scared and . . . owwww!" Her hand went to her forehead.

"What is it?"

"The men!" She gasped. "They've just sent a double command to return. And, Jakkin, it hurts. I have to . . ." She stopped talking and a blank look crept into her eyes. She began to turn around.

Jakkin grabbed her by the waist and pulled her underwater. She struggled violently against him and her right hand smacked his chin. He let her go and she burst up into the air, spluttering and gasping.

"Jakkin, that wasn't funny!" She stopped, put her hand over his mouth, and stared at him. "My head," she whispered, "it's crackling. And . . . and I can't hear them anymore. I'm all alone in here!"

"It'll last for only a little while," he said, glancing quickly over his shoulder at the men and waving at them. They looked puzzled. He turned back, whispering frantically. "Listen, Akki, I don't think they'll come into the water unless they have to.

Remember, they've got only the sendings, no words. They wouldn't want to lose it. So tell me quickly what you know. I didn't see anything but the Place of Men. It's nothing but a dreary cave where they pick out Ore and turn it into molten metal. But *metal*, Akki. Do you realize what that means?"

She nodded, lacing her fingers together.

"I didn't even know much about the dragons or these caves until today. Or tonight. Or whatever worm-eaten time it is."

Akki took a deep breath and her words came to him in a rush. "I don't know much more. The Place of Women is filled with women and children, though there are only a few babies and a good number of them are sickly. They seem to spend a lot of time preparing food. And weaving. And making clothing."

Jakkin thought a minute. "What about the food? Where does it come from?"

"Come from? I don't . . . oh, I see what you mean, Jakkin. If they're growing food—or gathering it—they have to have access to the outside."

Jakkin nodded.

"But where?"

"And," he added, "how do *we* get there, wherever there is?"

Puddling her hand in the water, Akki sighed. "Jakkin . . ." she said.

He waited.

"Something else. It's been puzzling me a lot. Those babies. They cry like ordinary babies, you know—sounds. But the older ones, the toddlers, they don't make any noise at all, even when they fall down taking their first steps. They just sprawl on the cave floor and send unhappy-feeling patterns. Somehow something—or someone—teaches them to forget language and use only their minds. *And I don't know what it is!"* Her hands ran through the tangles of her hair.

Jakkin reached over and took her hands in his. Just as they touched, the crackle in his mind stopped and he could feel her puzzlement and fear.

"Quick!" he said. "Duck down into the water again." But it was too late. The men on the ledge had been joined by Makk. Their sending, strengthened by linking hands, was too strong to be disobeyed.

"COME. COME. COME."

Jakkin's last coherent thought was that he'd heard that command before. Then he took Akki's hand, and they walked out of the lake to stand before the waiting men.

16

For two sleep periods—Jakkin couldn't be sure they were actual nights—they'd been forced to remain by the dragon's side. They slept on the stone floor by her stall without even the comfort of grass pallets. Hulking, expressionless guards watched over them, ready to slap them if they tried to speak out loud. Anytime Jakkin tried a sending he was painfully aware that the guards were listening in, painfully because they often doubled their sendings, leaving him with an aching head. He and Akki were reduced to passing looks to remind themselves that they were not stooping, silent cave dwellers.

In her frustration Akki began a frantic round of nursing that was at first welcomed by the dragon, then tolerated, and at last shaken away with tail thumpings and fierce houghing. Jakkin, in his turn, groomed the dragon until her scales were polished to a shine that even old Likkarn, Old Likk-and-Spittle, would have admired. But finally the dragon shook him off too.

When the dragon started stretching her neck out to the fullest, Jakkin knew she was well again and ready to lay her eggs. Neck stretching was an unconscious gesture left over from the days when dragons had scouted for danger in the mountain caves where they gave birth. Sarkkhan had told him that.

Always before when Jakkin had been near a layer, he'd been caught up in her sendings, violent maelstroms of color. But this dragon's sendings were in black, white, and gray, and while they were no less violent, Jakkin found himself outside the waves of her emotions rather than caught up in them. However, the cave people, whose own sendings were as colorless, seemed to be buffeted by the dragon's wild sendings and they fled the cavern as soon as she began, leaving Jakkin and Akki alone.

They stayed, partly because they were delighted to be shed of the guards, but primarily because Akki feared there might still be problems with the newly healed canal.

"It's too soon," she whispered, even though there was no one else in the room. "The eggs might tear open the scabs."

"That'll be a mess," Jakkin said.

"And painful," Akki added.

As they watched, the pressure in the dragon's birth canal began to send waves rolling up under the sternum and along the heavy stomach muscles. She reared up, her head scraping the rounded ceiling. Fluttering her wings, she pressed them to her sides, the edges touching her belly. Jakkin could see her earflaps vibrating steadily as she slowly settled back down.

"Easy, easy, my beauty," he murmured, remembering with a sudden shudder the last time he'd spoken these same words to a laying hen. It had been to Heart's Blood, and the eggs she'd dropped contained Sssargon, Sssasha, and the triplets.

Akki's head snapped up and she grinned. "The triplets," she whispered. "Lizard lumps, how I miss them."

Jakkin didn't even mind that she'd read his thoughts, but he pointed to his mouth. "Use words," he said.

"Where do you think they are now?"

"Who?"

"The triplets."

"Outside." He sighed.

"I wish we were outside," Akki said.

He touched her hand, stroking it with his fingers. "We *will* be soon. I promise."

And then the dragon's panting began, in and out, in and out; the ragged breathing filled the cavern and settled over them like a heavy mist. They stopped talking as the rhythm enveloped them.

The dragon heaved herself to her feet and backed out of the stall, pushing Akki to the floor and squashing Jakkin against the wall. Mindlessly the worm stomped around the room three times, as if searching for something. Her frantic pacing disturbed the two dragons in the outer stalls, and they houghed at her. She responded by whipping her tail back and forth.

At last she found a shallow depression filled with sand at the far end of the cavern. Eyeing it for a moment, she tested it with a claw. Evidently it satisfied her, for she squatted over it and began to push down. Eggs popped out between her back legs, cascading continuously into the sandy nest for the better part of several hours.

Higher and higher the pile of eggs grew until at last the pile was so high, she had to stand to finish the job. As she did a sticky yellow-white afterbirth tinged slightly with red trickled out of the canal, coating the eggs and binding them together.

"See the blood," Akki whispered to Jakkin. "Some of the scabs must have come off."

The dragon shook herself all over, stepped over the pyramid of eggs, and waddled slowly back to the stall, where she began cleaning herself.

Jakkin pulled Akki out of the stall just in time. They were as drained as if they'd done all the hard work of laying themselves. Akki slumped against the cave wall and fell asleep. Jakkin sat down next to her and was soon snoring gently. Their dreams were full of color and light and the smell of the open air.

They woke well before the dragon, who was in the comalike sleep that followed egg laying. Jakkin knew that was how the first dragons had been captured, during the vulnerable aftermath of birth.

As they woke they were buffeted by new storms, not from the dragon but from many individual human sendings. Surprised, they looked around the cavern. It was filled with silent men, women, and children jostling one another for a look at the eggs. The most surprising thing of all was that they were all dressed in white robes, a costume oddly unsuited to their heavy bodies.

Makk left the crowd and came over to them, holding out his hands in a gesture of greeting. *"Good. Much good."* Then he waved his hands at the white-robed people behind him.

What followed his wave was such a clamor in the mind that Jakkin could think of it only as a cheer. It made him shiver with its intensity, and gave him the worst headache he'd ever had.

As quickly as it had arisen, the silent cheer stopped, but the ache above his eyes continued. Jakkin rubbed at his forehead but it didn't help.

"Come!" Makk's sending was both an invitation and a command.

Jakkin stood and pulled Akki up after him, and they joined the crowd surging out of the cavern down a long, straight tunnel and into a small, niched cave, where they were helped into white robes of their own.

Jakkin turned to Akki, mouthing "What's going on?"

She shrugged, pointed to her head, and rubbed her left temple with a finger.

Before he could answer, they were rushed away again, moving like part of an underground river racing through the tunnels into yet another cave.

This cave was enormous and vaulted, its ceiling strung with lanterns. Tapestries hung along the walls, the pictures on them primitive but clearly showing dragons and children superimposed upon one another. Long wooden tables sided by benches covered most of the floor space.

Jakkin was pushed toward a bench and made to sit, strangers on either side of him. Across the way was Akki. The table was piled high with dishes of steaming stews and salads, boiled mushrooms both gray and white, and cups of a liquid the color of fresh blood.

There was no ceremony. Just as in the bondhouse, everyone reached out for whatever he or she wanted. The clattering of dishes and the banging of hands on the table contrasted strangely with the wordlessness of the people in the room.

After so many days of limited fare, the sight of so much food was overwhelming. Jakkin could feel saliva pooling in his mouth. A strange smell pervaded the room, and it took him a moment to realize it came from the tallow candles set at the table ends. Hungry as he was, Jakkin suddenly felt sick to his stomach. The only thing that could make that much tallow would be dragon fat. Even though his plate was piled high with a variety of inviting foods, he no longer felt like eating. His head ached still, his stomach revolted at the smells. He shook his head.

The man on the right clapped Jakkin on the shoulder before turning back eagerly to his food.

Jakkin sat back and made his mind a blank. Slowly he built up a wall, concentrating on each block until it was as high as his head. He felt rather than heard someone standing in the front of the room and he looked up.

Makk had his hands raised above his head in a kind of benediction, fingers semaphoring to all who watched him. Jakkin raised himself carefully over his mental wall to listen, and Makk's sending came to him full force:

"Eggs are high. Now we eat. Now we sleep. Not-now we watch hatching. Not-now we count eggs. Time we celebrate. Time we praise. Time we birth again. Blood to blood."

All around the room people were leaping to their feet, raising their hands overhead.

"Blood to blood," their sendings repeated. For the first time a river of color, bright red, washed through their black-and-white minds. *"Blood to blood."*

In the end only Jakkin and Akki, across the table from him, remained seated. Akki was weeping silently, tears channeling down her cheeks. Jakkin hissed at her and she opened her eyes and stared at him. He sent one word across their bridged minds: *"Why?"*

She bit her lip, then whispered, "Oh, Jakkin, I'm afraid. I don't know why, but I'm so horribly afraid."

Suddenly Jakkin caught her feelings and they rushed through him, pushing out the bloody sendings, his headache, and everything else except that fear. And he knew he was afraid too. It only made it worse that he didn't know why.

17

As Makk said, they ate and slept and then ate again, an enormous display of gluttony that made Jakkin so sick he refused to go back in the dining room.

The watch was set: three men and three women at a time, with a child between them, waited by the nest. Jakkin supposed they were there to guard the eggs from any flikka, though the caverns had seemed curiously without life. *And* to report when the eggs started hatching.

Jakkin and Akki were dragged along to make up one of the watch teams. They kept their vigil for less than an hour, or so it seemed, squatting back on their heels and staring silently at the now-hardened pyramid. Jakkin's stomach was still queasy and he wondered if he were *clutched,* which is how trainers linked to a dragon often felt when the hen was laying. But this wasn't his dragon and he was hardly linked with her, at least any more than the rest were. He suspected it was just plain fear. And what was that fear? It had something to do with the bloody sendings, that much he knew. And something about the way the cave people greedily devoured their dragon stew. But he'd had friends like that at the nursery and they'd never frightened him. It was just a feeling he had. And Akki, he knew, felt the same.

When his watch was over Jakkin stood with the rest of the white-robed guardians, but instead of filing down the tunnel with them he moved over to the dragon's stall. She was getting restless in her sleep and he knew she'd be waking before long.

Akki came over to the stall and touched his shoulder. They stood that way as the new watchers entered the cavern to take their turns.

The silence in the cave was unbearable. Jakkin was ready to say something aloud, whatever the consequences, when the dragons in the far stalls began to rock back and forth in place. Jakkin welcomed the creak of bone, the muffled thud of the dragon feet. The rhythm was compelling and he began to sway with them.

And then the dragon sleeping by his feet awoke. Shaking her head from side to side, she stood and backed out of the stall. The watchers at the nest scattered as she moved purposefully toward the pyramid of eggs.

Stopping by the nest, she lowered her head slowly until her nose rested on the topmost egg. For a moment she didn't move, then houghed a mighty breath out through her nose. The wet, warm breath touched the eggs and a kind of vapor surrounded the top three or four. For a moment the hard shells seemed almost translucent. Jakkin imagined he could see into them and judge the contents. Then the moment passed. The dragon rolled the topmost egg off the pile and onto the floor. It was a miracle it did not break, but the hard elastic shell was almost impenetrable from the outside. Only the hatchling within, with the birth bump of horn on its nose, could easily crack open the shell.

Soon the floor by the nest was littered with the cream-colored eggs. There seemed to be nearly a hundred.

A babble of sendings filtered through Jakkin's concentration and he looked around. The cavern was fast filling with people jostling for position; the children pushed to the front. Unmoved, the dragon continued her work.

Touching each egg in turn, she shoved them around with her lanceae, the twin nails on the front of her foot, almost as if she were counting them, as if she knew already which eggs held live hatchlings and which were just slime-filled decoys for the flikka and drakk.

She tapped an egg that lay close to her right foot. *Tap. Tap-tap.* She paused. *Tap-tap.*

There was a tiny echo from inside the egg. *Tap-tap.*

She touched the egg again with a more vigorous stroke. *TAP!*

A thin dark line formed on the shell, the barest whisper of a crack.

Jakkin let out a breath.

Suddenly the line became a wider crack, zigzagging like an old river around the smaller end of the egg.

The dragon gave the egg a final tap and it split apart. In the larger half lay a crumpled form, curled tightly around itself. It was the color of scum and was covered with a yellow-green fluid.

The hen dragon overturned the shell and the wrinkled hatchling stumbled blindly onto the cave floor, its eyes still sealed shut with the egg fluids. She gave it a perfunctory lick, then turned her attention to the inside of the shell, which she cleaned with her rough-ridged tongue. When all the fluids were gone she went back to the hatchling, licking it clean. Once free of the fluids that had coated its overlarge wings and head, the hatchling flopped down to sleep. The hen ignored it and once again picked through the eggs.

Seven times she tapped an egg, once biting an egg open with her under-tongue growth. In four of the shells were live hatchlings. Two of the eggs contained deformed dragons, one that trembled for a minute in the air before it died, the other long dead and stinking. The third shell held nothing but a bright yellow yolk with a coin-sized spot of blood in its center. She gobbled the yolk down eagerly.

When it was clear the Great Mother was through picking over the eggs and had fallen back into sleep, the crowd surged forward to clean up the nest and its scattered contents. Each person took an egg or a handful of sand as a souvenir. The dragon was shooed back to her stall with her hatchlings. Then the floor was swept up by the same two women who had been with the dragon from the first. It all happened so quickly, it was as if the hatching had never occurred.

Jakkin was shocked that the cave people had not let the mother dragon crack open and eat the rest of the eggs. There might even be a singleton, an egg that opens late with a slowly forming baby dragon in it. Every nursery bonder knew how important it was for the mother dragon to get those extra rations to replace the fluids and protein she had lost in the hatching. How else could she recover?

Yet even as he worried about the dragon's condition, Jakkin had to smile. The five new hatchlings, wrinkled, ugly, and ungainly, were already nestled by their sleeping mother's side, their butter-soft baby claws pushing against one another in their sleep.

18

How long they sat by the dragon's stall, half dozing in the dim light, Jakkin didn't know. What wakened him was a rumbling noise that began as a low growl and rose steadily into an angry roar. He looked around and couldn't see anything, but an uneasiness invaded his mind, a misty sending that suddenly resolved itself into a tunnel-shaped blackness shot through with familiar gray rainbows.

Jakkin's head jerked up and Akki whispered, "That's Auricle. She's here. Why didn't we notice before?"

Jakkin shook his head. "She never sent anything before."

"And we were too worried about the egg laying," Akki added.

They stood and followed the sending to the side stalls where two dragons were rocking nervously from foot to foot.

"Which one is Auricle?" Akki asked.

Jakkin sent a pattern of blues like lazy rivers meandering across the dark sendings from both dragons. "I'm not sure," he said to Akki. "We never actually *saw* her. It was too dark in the tunnels."

"And I was too scared."

"Me too." He laughed aloud. "Me too."

"So, which one?"

Jakkin sent Auricle's name, bound about with colorful rainbows, and the larger of the two dragons, the pale red, raised her
head to stare back at him.

"Not-man?" Her large dark eyes grew larger still.

"Akki, it's the red. She's *got* to be Heart's Blood's cousin."

"Don't start that again, Jakkin. There's no way to know. Not
for sure. And she's not your dragon anyway. She belongs here, in
the cave."

"Not-man?" the red dragon sent again.

"What is it?" Jakkin whispered, molding the question into a
sending as well. But no sooner had he sent it than a different
sending filled his mind, so loud his head hurt with it.

"COME. COME. COME."

The rumbling noise and the sending seemed to blend together
until the command was irresistible, and Akki and Jakkin stumbled toward the tunnel entrance. But the dragons, cuffed as they
were by iron bonds at neck and foot, didn't leave their stalls, only
started rocking again. The sleeping mother dragon stirred uneasily, lifting her head for a moment in a dazed fashion before
sinking back into her stupor.

At the entrance Jakkin could see movement down the tunnel
and soon he could make out the figures of Makk and six of his
men hauling an enormous wheeled cart. Jakkin put his hand out
and dragged Akki back inside the cavern as the men pulled the
cart through the arch.

Stripped of their ceremonial robes and wearing only leather
shorts, the men's arm muscles bulged and flattened, then bulged
again as they tugged the cart over the uneven cavern floor. Behind the cart, pushing, were another half dozen men similarly

stripped down. Beyond them Jakkin could make out the entire
company of cave people still dressed in their white robes. The
women were now garlanded with strings of dried chikkberries
and warden's hearts and some kind of yellow-centered flowers.
Five in the front carried naked infants in their arms, babies
whose heads were crowned with circlets of leaves.

As the cart rumbled into the cavern Makk directed the men
toward the stall where the sleeping dragon once again tried to
shake herself out of her stupor, but the lack of extra birth fluids
had already taken its toll and she could scarcely move.

The five women came forward, walked in front of the cart,
and into the sleeping dragon's stall. The first touched the dragon
on the flank. Her sending was restrained but perfectly clear.

"Great Mother, my child, your child, be one."

She bent down and picked up one of the hatchlings with her
free hand. It was the same size as her infant, small enough to fit
comfortably into the crook of her right arm.

The second woman entered the dragon's stall and touched the
hen on the shoulder.

"Great Mother, my child, your child, be one."

"Jakkin, I don't like this." Akki's mouth was right against his
ear. He put his hand up as if to silence her but never took his
eyes off the unfolding drama.

The third woman touched the dragon on the head, the fourth
over the heart, and the fifth placed her hand on the dragon's
belly. Each woman's sending was the same and each, in turn,
picked up a hatchling and cradled it against her breasts.

Akki whispered frantically in his ear, "They're going to kill the
hatchlings, Jakkin, I know it." Her breath was hot. "What kind
of people are they?"

Jakkin shook his head. What kind of people? He remembered

his own nursery's culling day, when unsuitable hatchlings had been taken from the screaming hens and sent off to the Stews. What kind of people were these men and women of the cave? What kind of people were *all* the people of Austar?

The women holding the hatchlings turned, walked out of the stall in a line, and with slow, measured steps walked across the cavern to a small holding pen of wood and stone. They placed the baby dragons in it and closed the gate.

Akki let out a relieved sigh that almost deafened Jakkin, then slipped her hand into his, masking her feelings behind a carefully constructed wall he couldn't penetrate. Silently they continued to watch.

The robeless men crowded into the stall, six on either side of the sleeping dragon and Makk by her tail, holding a plaited net. The men at the dragon's front rolled her onto her back and Makk slung the net down at their feet, then spread the net where she'd been. When they let her go she rocked back on top of the net.

Then the men in the back did the same and Makk pulled the net through so that it spread across the entire stall floor. When the dragon was settled again each man grabbed a handful of net and, on a mental signal, heaved her toward the cart. It took a lot of grunting and straining, and more than once a man let out a mental curse that struck Jakkin's mind with the force of a hammer blow. Though he'd heard many curses in the nursery, they'd never made him physically ill before. Jakkin rubbed his temples, trying to ease away the pain.

At last the dragon was positioned on the cart, her tail dragging off the end. Makk and his twelve helpers took up the rope at the front. Six robed men came around the back to push. The five women carrying infants each helped pick up the dragon's tail so that it wouldn't scrape along the floor. Then they began to haul the cart and dragon out of the cavern.

Jakkin had no idea of their destination, though he feared it was the pile of white bones at the tunnel's end. He sent a picture of that pile to Akki, and she squeezed his hand. Puzzled, he looked at her. She was smiling. Turning her head toward him, she whispered, "The bone pile is near the entrance, Jakkin. We could escape."

He knew she was right, yet something about the ceremony they'd just witnessed kept him from celebrating. The chanting women, the white-robed men all seemed destined for some dark purpose, and he followed them hand in hand with Akki because they knew no other way.

It was hard, sweaty, backbreaking work, but Makk and his men never faltered. Surprisingly, none of the other men offered a hand. It was as if towing the dragon were a singular honor that only certain men were given, though Jakkin couldn't figure out why. The rest of the people, who trailed behind the cart, seemed enveloped in a carnival atmosphere, smiling and waving their arms, their sendings shot through with unexpected colors, though their silence lent a bizarre note to the whole proceedings. The only noise was the constant rumble of the cartwheels broken by an occasional high, piping cry of one of the infants in its mother's arms.

Just when Jakkin was beginning to believe there was no end to the journey, only the parade through a maze of tunnels, he saw a pinpoint of bright light ahead, beyond the surging crowd and beyond the cart with its comatose burden. Then the pinpoint became larger, irised open until it filled him completely. Only then did he realize he was not just seeing the spot of light but receiving it as a sending as well.

It took him another moment to understand that the light wasn't torchlight or lanterns or the light from phosphorescent mosses. He threw his hands up over his eyes to help filter out the intense brightness as he continued forward with the crowd. When he finally pulled his hands away he saw they were in a large meadow dotted with copses of trees. The meadow was entirely surrounded by the steep, sloping sides of the mountain, as if they were at the bottom of an enormous bowl.

It was night. What Jakkin had thought was a single bright light was really the pale glow of the sand-colored moons, Akka and Akkhan. He'd been so used to the dim caves that the twin moons seemed uncomfortably bright. Squinting, he stared up at them. A dark figure swept across Akkhan's face. A wild dragon, he thought.

And then, as if in a dream, came the rainbow pattern he knew so well, filling him with hope.

"Sssargon waits. Sssargon hunts. Sssargon . . ."

Then the sending was gone, blotted out by the closer patterns of the people around him and the dark rumblings of the cart.

The cart moved more easily now, along well-worn ruts, toward a great stone enclosure in the center of the meadow. The ring reminded Jakkin vaguely of some of the country Pits, with their stone seats around a center maw.

The men drew the cart through a stone archway and into the center of the ring, where, with a ceremonial heave, they hauled the dragon off the cart. She lay where they dropped her, panting and blinking sleepily up at the light.

Herded into their seats by the crowd, Akki and Jakkin sat next to one another but didn't touch, afraid that their thoughts would thereby be doubly broadcast to the cave folk. And soon Jakkin's attention left Akki and was focused on the ring.

He wondered if there was to be a fight. If so, there'd be nothing but a straightforward slaughter, for the hen could barely get her head up. In fact, if she weren't fed soon, she'd die. He didn't like the way she was breathing, and *everyone* knew that a hen right after egg laying and hatching needed extra rations. The irony of it wasn't lost on him—that he and Akki had worked so hard to save her and were now helplessly going to watch her die. He thought about that a moment. He *wouldn't* be helpless. Shaking himself loose of the crowd-induced torpor, he started to stand and protest. But as he stood everyone else stood, too, as if reacting to some signal he'd not even registered.

Once again in their white robes, Makk and his men entered the ring and formed a tight circle around the dragon, as if guarding her. The five garlanded women, infants in arms, stood by the dragon's tail.

The familiar chant began again. *"COME. COME. COME."*

For a long moment no one moved except the hen, whose tail beat a feeble tattoo on the ground.

Then, from the left side, through the stone arch, marched a figure in dark red. Her robe was stiff and fell in peculiar rigid folds from her shoulders. A cowl covered her head, a veil her face. Only her eyes showed, ringed with black paint. She carried a long white stick in her right hand.

Coming to the circle of men, the woman stopped until they moved apart, then walked to the dragon's head, where she raised her hands above her.

"Great Mother," she sent, and the people echoed it, a dark black-and-white picture of a towering dragon form that seemed to shimmer in the mind from so many sendings. *"Where your*

children cradled, cradle mine." She brought her hands slashing down toward the dragon's exposed neck.

In that instant Jakkin knew what it was she carried: a forefoot bone with the nails still intact. Only a dragon's nail could slice efficiently through dragon scale, though the underneck links were the tenderest part.

Blood gouted from the dragon's neck and covered the woman's robe and cowl, staining it a deeper red. The hot, acidic blood spattered on the rocks below and splattered on the woman's hands. It must have burned her, pocking her wrists and fingers, but she never dropped her weapon. At the very moment of the cut she broadcast a high, piercing sending of triumph and light. The answering image from both the dying dragon and the people around the ring was a tidal wave of red: bright red, blood red, an ocean of it that threatened to drown them all.

Jakkin closed his eyes, hoping to shut out the sight, but the sending went on and on, replaying the scene endlessly in his horrified mind.

Minutes later the woman in red cut open the dragon's belly and one by one the women laid their infants in the dragon's birth chamber, closing the flap of skin over them to ensure the babies' invulnerability to cold and to open their minds to the linkings of dragons and men.

Akki wept openly through it all, but Jakkin forced himself to remain dry-eyed. He felt hardly anything but guilt, for as soon as the bloody sendings from the crowd had ended, his own bloody memories had begun. He remembered, before the change, the three dragons in his life who had died because of him. The great stud Blood Brother, killed in the nursery, because Jakkin had been careless. He remembered Brother as he last saw him, in a hindfoot rise, pulling his leather halter out of the stall ring and screaming his defiance over Jakkin's prone body until Likkarn brought him down with a barn stinger. Then there was the pit fighter S'Blood, that Jakkin allowed to get badly wounded in a fight. He remembered S'Blood's last moments, protesting groggily in the slaughterhouse Stews as the steward, in one economical movement, shot him through the ear while Jakkin and Master Sarkkhan watched, helpless, from the walkway above. And then there was Heart's Blood. *Heart's Blood.* That memory was the worst of all. The great red towering majestically above Jakkin and Akki, taking the shots meant for them, death blossoming on her chest like a hideous bloody flower.

No more, he thought. *I will allow no more. Not Auricle. Not the new hatchlings. Not if I have to die to prevent it.*

the
fighters

19

Jakkin dreamed of it all that night, the woman in the blood-stiffened cloak so triumphantly slashing the throat of the weakened dragon, then carving open the worm's belly, and the five infants being cradled in the birth chamber. His dreams were as red as the blood that had covered the babies when they were lifted out of their fleshy nest, changed forever by their contact with the dead dragon's body. In his dream the dragon was no longer the unnamed brown that he and Akki had saved for the knife but his much-mourned Heart's Blood. And the infants all wore his own face. He dreamed he was drowning in the blood, and when he woke up he was covered with sweat.

He'd fallen asleep in the bowl of meadow along with Makk and the rest of the people, all of them exhausted by the awful ceremony and its equally bloody aftermath. But, unlike the others, he and Akki hadn't feasted on the raw dragon meat, hadn't helped carve away flesh from bone with nail and knife and teeth. Instead they'd watched in horror as the bones, still spotted with the bloody bits of meat, had been piled in a pyramid atop the cart, a pyramid that made mockery of the eggs the dragon had so recently laid. They didn't even need the wild sendings of the crowd to tell them that soon the cart would transport the bones to the great white pile far off in the caves where scavengers would do the rest.

Akki, eyes swollen from weeping, had turned to run and hide somewhere in the tunnels. Her sending was an agony that flashed through to him despite the blood-red frenzies of the crowd.

"We can't go now," Jakkin had whispered to her. "Think, Akki, think. If we run now, we leave Auricle. She'll die the same way. We let Heart's Blood die. We let the brown. We can't let Auricle go like this."

She'd turned toward him, nodding reluctantly.

He'd put his arms around her. "We'll stay and watch and plan. We've got only one chance to get it right."

Akki had kept her face hidden against his chest, but Jakkin had borne witness to the rest of the ceremony. Then they'd fallen asleep in one another's arms.

But because they had not taken part in the horrible feast, Jakkin and Akki woke early, Akki first, pulling at Jakkin's arm until he woke covered with sweat, the sun high overhead. The smell of the carnage was still heavy in the early-morning air.

Akki, her eyes like dark bruises, turned toward him. Jakkin concentrated on those eyes, trying to forget his dreams.

"I feel so . . . so dirty," Akki whispered.

"I think I can get us back to the bath lake," he said with confidence, though his traitor mind sent uneasiness and confusion. "At least I can try."

They sneaked away from the sleeping people, careful not to step on outflung arms. It helped that they had fallen asleep on

the edge of the crowd. Grabbing a torch that was still spluttering
in its metal sconce, they plunged into the inviting darkness of
the tunnel. Akki went on ahead, thankful to quit the meadow
light, but Jakkin turned back for a moment. For the first time he
looked beyond the crowd and the bloody altar and noticed carefully cultivated fields around the meadow's rim. His mind
worked furiously. Could those fields have been worked by the
same people who had torn apart a dragon in an hour of bloody
worship? The acres of painstaking hoeings did not seem to be-
long to a folk who savaged a dragon hen just a day after she'd
laid her eggs to their silent approval. He turned back onto the
dark winding path into the mountain's heart, remembering his
own home, a place where dragon breeders ate dragon steaks and
men linked with dying beasts reveled in their cries in the Stews.
People—people were a puzzle. He guessed he preferred the dragons.

"Akki," he called out, relieved to be able to use his full voice
again. "Akki, wait for me!"

They took several wrong turnings and had to back up three
times, but it was Akki who noticed it first, at a juncture.

"Look, Jakkin, the phosphorescence isn't just haphazard.
There's a pattern. Five lines here." She ran her hand over the
nubbly moss and for a moment her finger glowed. A disem-
bodied white finger pointed. "And three over there."

Jakkin looked. She was right. "That explains how they can run
through the tunnels and never get lost." He laughed, holding an
imaginary conversation with himself. "And where do you live,
Master Makk? Why on number three, past five, second cave to
your right!"

"So if we can remember the number patterns, we can find our way around," Akki said.

Just as she finished speaking they rounded a turning in the number five tunnel and stumbled into a small cavern with a lake at its center.

"I said I'd find it!"

Akki shook her head. "I don't think you found *it*—I think you found another one." She handed the torch to Jakkin, who set it carefully against the wall. "These caves must be riddled with lakes."

"You may be right," Jakkin agreed. "This one doesn't have the ledge where the guards stood."

"I'm always right." She laughed and stripped off her robe. She was wearing her own clothes underneath. Before he could react she'd waded in. When the water was as high as her shoulders, she stopped and turned around. "Come on, Jakkin. Why are you so . . . ?" She took one more step back and disappeared under the water, her mouth still open to speak.

Jakkin thought she was joking and waited for her to resurface, laughing. After a moment he began to get worried. He knew she couldn't swim. A moment more and he ripped off his own robe and dived in. The water was icy cold and he was afraid it was going to be pitch-black underneath. To his surprise, when he opened his eyes the water was dark green and, the farther down he went, a piercing light green shot through with gold. Ahead he could see a dark, slim shadow. It had to be Akki. He swam as fast as he could toward that black spot and at last he could make her out, arms above her head, legs limp, her hair spun out around her head like a web.

He grabbed a handful of her hair and drew her toward him. Her eyes were open and staring, her mouth a black O. Putting his right arm around her waist, he started to kick upward when he realized he wasn't really sure, in this crystalline world, which way was up and which was down. But trusting to memory, he went away from the light, paddling desperately one-handed toward the black wall.

They shot up and out of the water. He gasped for air, but Akki did not. He dragged her toward the shore and, when he finally got his footing, hauled her up onto the rock. He knew little about healing, less about someone who had almost drowned. All he had was his body's desperate knowledge.

"Oh, Akki, please. *Please!*" he cried. "Not now. Not when we've escaped." The echo of his voice was dampened by his water-filled ears. He couldn't reach her by a sending for there was only that crackle in his mind, the water-induced static. He pulled her close to him in a last mindless embrace and the pressure of his body against hers caused water to spew from her mouth.

Frantically he turned her over onto her stomach and pushed against her back, reasoning that he might be able to pump more water from her that way. Water drained from her mouth and nose, but still she didn't take a breath. He pushed and pushed until he could coax no more out, until his arms ached, then turned her over and stared.

Her eyes were closed. Her mouth was slack. There was a reddening bruise on her cheek from the stone.

"Oh, Akki, *please*," he cried again. "Take my breath. *Please!*" He put his mouth on hers, as if he could force air into her, and blew. Once. Twice. Three times.

And then, as if rejecting his breath, she coughed, a frothy rough hacking that sent both breath and water back into his mouth. He gagged. She opened her eyes and they were like water-filmed stones. Then life seemed to spark in them again slowly. She coughed once more and Jakkin hugged her, burying his face against her neck. He didn't want her to see him cry.

"Oh, Akki," he whispered hoarsely, his lips against her cold skin, "I thought you were dead."

"Not . . . not dead yet," she whispered back, her voice unnaturally low. "But awfully wet. And cold."

Tenderly he wrapped her robe about her shoulders. "Don't move," he said. "Just get warm. And get your breath back. There's something I have to check out. But I'll be back."

He turned and dived into the water, an inelegant splashing. Just before his head went under his mind cleared and he could feel her sending, still pale but clear:

"Where would I go without *you*, Jakkin?"

20

As he went down, down, down toward the piercing green light, Jakkin concentrated only on his swimming. He was an instinctual but untrained swimmer and had never gone any long distances before. Most of his swimming had been of the splash-and-wade variety, done in the water that threaded through the oasis where he'd raised Heart's Blood. But he pulled strongly with his arms, kept his feet kicking steadily, and headed into the center of the green light. He *counted* on that light—it had to be a way out.

Just when he thought his lungs would burst the green turned a brilliant white and he followed it up and into the air. He grabbed great gulps of breath and his chest heaved up and down. When his eyes were no longer water-filmed he saw he was in a cavern of green-white crystals. Overhead and on the cave walls were strange, faceted rocks that pulsed with light. Above the water, rainbow shadows danced and shimmered. Then he realized that instead of being in a lake he was in an eddying river whose slow-moving current was carrying him along. He paddled in desultory fashion, letting the river do the work, and in this way rounded a great curve. Suddenly an enormous opening was before him. It was as high as the nursery stud barn and opened on to endless sky.

The water carried him through. He turned over and floated along on his back, looking up into the clear blue Austarian sky where a black dot was scripting an elliptic message. His mind still crackled with the water's static, so there was no way he could receive a sending that would tell him if that dot was a dragon—or a copter. He flipped back over onto his stomach, took three strong strokes, and clambered out onto a bank whose grass came right down into the water.

From where he stood, shaking himself like a dragon just emerged from a bath, he could see that the river wound on for another couple hundred meters, and then disappeared precipitously, as if the end were suddenly sheered off. There was a constant low deep sound, which seemed at once comforting and ominous. He wondered about it, but it wasn't like any sound he'd ever heard.

Behind him the mountain climbed straight up, as if a second mountain stood atop the first, its dark rocks broken and ugly. On the other side of the river was a grassy slope similar to the one he stood on, and beyond it a sheer drop. He could see a stretch of desert land below with scattered green-black clumps of trees. And even farther on there was a black snaky line he guessed was a river, perhaps even the Narakka.

He became aware of the untrammeled grass between his toes, cool and tickling. Smiling at last, he threw himself facedown and let the strong familiar earth smell surround him.

But all the while he was thinking furiously, questions boiling up inside. How was he to get Akki, who could not swim, through the water to this blue and green haven? How could he convince a dragon already beginning to swell with eggs to swim to an unknown and unknowable destination? How could he hold both girl and worm through the terrifying moments underwater when none of them would be able to link minds? And, above all, how could he do it so that the cave people didn't know their plans ahead of time or follow them into this light and open place?

Shaking his head, Jakkin let the sun warm and dry him. Slowly his mind cleared of the static, and as it did he felt it invaded by a faraway sending, faded but familiar:

"Sssargon rides. Sssargon turns. Sssargon . . ."

Jakkin chuckled to himself, waiting for the dragon to become aware of his presence. Then as the dragon monologue continued unabated, realization dawned on Jakkin. Sssargon simply didn't hear him. He, Jakkin, was broadcasting none of his feelings. The habits he had learned in his long days deep in the cave held. Without even worrying about it, without working at visualizing a wall or a curtain or a fence, he could now cloak his feelings. Thankfully he opened his mind and let out a whoop of color. "Sssargon!" his sending shouted. "Sssargon, shut up! And Sssargon—come here!"

The dot did a complete loop-de-loop and started toward him, its sendings blasting out a parade of patterns—reds, golds, purples. In its wake there came four other sendings, related yet individual. The hatchlings, Heart's Blood's five, had all heard him and were on their way.

They nearly broke two of his ribs and fairly suffocated him once they had landed, crowding around in boisterous delight. Sssasha had to buffet the triplets away from him with a broad sweep of her tail. And Sssargon, undaunted by their teasing, continued his commentary throughout the reunion, a color-filled drone that soon had them all chuckling.

"Sssargon laughs. Sssargon feels joy."

At last Jakkin caught his breath and cleared his mind. He looked carefully at the five, all of whom seemed overgrown after the stunted, dull dragons of the cave. He patted Sssasha's nose with its splotch of gold, then opened his mind to them slowly, like a storyteller beginning a tale. He made them feel the low, dark inside of the mountain caves and the low, dark minds of the cave's damaged inhabitants. He pictured the work details, the reunion with Akki, the healing of the dragon, and the silent, steady laying of the eggs. Then, with a kind of mental drumroll, he pounded out the rest of the story, ending with the great gout of blood-red spewing over them all.

If dragons could weep, they wept. Crowding close to him, they rubbed against him in their need for comfort. Sssasha licked his ear carefully with her rough tongue.

Then Tri-ssskkette, with the mental equivalent of a sigh, sent a fluttering thought that flapped like the skin over her ears. *"Akki!"* She laced the picture of Akki in gold but the flutter lines kept breaking up the image. It was so plaintive, Jakkin reached over and hugged her around the neck.

"Akki," he said aloud, framing a simultaneous sending. Dragons recognized certain spoken words—names and specific objects—but the sendings were still necessary. *"Akki is under the mountain by the lake. I must go back. But thee will have a place in this ending, Tri—I promise thee that."*

The others pushed next to Tri-ssskkette, signaling their own willingness, and nearly knocked Jakkin over. He gave them each a pat on the nose.

"This is my plan, and it will be better to say it to thee now, for

once I am back in the water and under the mountain, I can send thee nothing."

"Nothing?" Sssargon was startled out of his self-involvement for a moment.

"Nothing," Jakkin repeated, both out loud and in a sending. *"The water stops all sendings."*

"Thee will be like other men then?" It was Sssasha who understood first.

"Almost." Jakkin nodded. *"But the people of the cave can send to dragons, and their sendings are strong. If thee feels it, Sssasha, if they call thee in this way"*—and he looked at them fiercely— *"COME, COME, COME, then thee must all pump thy wings and leave at once. For these are worm killers, bone stackers, blood drinkers. Thee must all leave Akki and me. No more of Heart's Blood's line must die for me. Do you understand?"*

They nodded their great heads up and down, up and down, in slow agreement, Sssasha first and then the triplets and, at the very last and reluctantly, Sssargon.

"Thee must wait here, ready to help. Thee must be my eyes and my ears." Then he told them what he planned, so shapeless a thing that even as he spoke and sent it, he wondered if it could possibly work.

When Jakkin had finished Sssargon put his nose against Jakkin's ear and blew a warm breath into it. Then he twisted his neck so that he was eye to eye with Jakkin. *"Sssargon hears. Sssargon be eyes."*

"We are thy ears, thy ears, thy ears." The triplets emphasized this by fluttering their earflaps outrageously. Jakkin rewarded them each with a chuck underneath the chin.

Then he turned to Sssasha. *"And thee, my beauty?"* he asked, touching the gold slash on her nose.

"I am thy heart, Jakkin," she sent. It was as clear and unambiguous as any sending the people of the cave could send, but it shimmered with light and with love, and he could read past, present, and future in it.

He turned, slid down the grassy slope back into the water. It seemed colder than before. As he started to stroke against the current, moving slowly upstream, he fought the impulse to turn and look back at the dragons. He needed every bit of strength for the difficult pull ahead. And he feared that if he saw them there he might not be able to go on. Water splashed up into his mouth and made him cough. His ears had begun to ring. The cold and the steady current sapped his fading strength even further. But he went on, one stroke after another, until he had battled his way back through the great opening in the mountainside and into the green crystal cave.

Treading water there, he looked about as if measuring something—the rocks, perhaps, or the walls, or his own fast-disappearing courage. Then through the static in his mind, as if it were a fresh sending, came the memory of Sssasha's words: *"I am thy heart, Jakkin."* Well, he would need the heart of a dragon to get through the rest of it. But for Sssasha, for all of them, for Akki and Auricle—and especially for Heart's Blood, who had sacrificed herself that they might live—he would be brave. Taking a deep breath, he dived down and swam swiftly and surely away from the light.

21

This time, tired as he was, Jakkin had been able to judge the amount of breath he needed, and he pulled himself through the ever-darkening water with growing confidence. Just as he began his ascent toward the green-black surface, something caught around his legs. Yanking and kicking, he brought the heavy object up to his eyes and saw, with horror, that it was one of the white robes.

His heart began to pound and his ears felt ready to burst. Fearing the worst—that the robe was Akki's and she'd *really* drowned this time—he pushed it away and watched it rise slowly. He swam desperately for the top, bursting up into the air, gulping mouthfuls into his exploding lungs, and then made for the shore. Rubbing the water from his eyes only seemed to make his vision worse, and he reminded himself to calm down. But when his eyes seemed clear at last he still had trouble seeing in the cave, and that was when he noticed the guttered torch lying in a puddle. The cavern was lit only by the water reflecting eerily on the walls. There was no sign of Akki. The robe in the water must have been his own.

He cursed himself for leaving her there so long, alone and unprotected, and his curses rose in volume and originality until he found himself screaming her name. The walls echoed crazily, bouncing the two syllables back and forth, as if playing with them. But there was no answer, and his static-filled mind could find no trace of any sendings.

"Akki!" he screamed again, starting down a tunnel.

Hearing a sound behind him, he turned abruptly. Something on the far side of the lake was rising up from the shallows.

"Shut up, Jakkin," she said. "Maybe we can't send, with all the static, but no one could miss your shouting. The walls are ringing with it!"

"Fewmets, Akki, I thought you were gone. I thought . . . I thought . . ." He found he could scarcely breathe.

She waded around the lake, careful to stay where the water was only knee-deep.

"What about what *I* thought, Jakkin," she said. "You were gone so long, I thought you were drowned. And I can't swim, so how could I rescue you? And then I thought that if you really had died, your body would float up. So I had hope that you'd found another way out. But I didn't know if I could follow." She hesitated. "But I always knew you'd come back for me if you could." She put her hand on his arm.

He shook it off angrily. "What were you doing underwater?" he asked. "You nearly scared me to death."

"Practicing!" she said lightly.

"Practicing? Practicing what?"

"That's a joke, Jakkin."

"I'm not in the mood for jokes."

"Well, you sure could use something to sweeten you."

He made a wry movement with his mouth.

"Actually it was the only way I could think to keep them from finding me. When they began that gathering call again, you know, 'COME, COME, COME,' I was so scared I wouldn't be able to resist it, I ducked down into the water. Even held my nose. And the chant stopped, just like that! Or at least I couldn't hear it anymore because of the crackling. Then I remembered both our robes were by the lake, so I came up for air and dragged them in with me. If Makk saw those, he'd figure out where we were easily." She smiled. "Smart, wasn't I?"

He was still not mollified. "You left the torch."

She looked over her shoulder at the guttered torch. "Oh, dragon's droppings. They'd have known anyway."

"Still," Jakkin said quietly, "it was awfully brave."

"It was awfully stupid," Akki insisted. "Don't patronize me, Jakkin. I've done brave things in my life. Don't forget I joined a rebel cell to spy on them. And I've lived out in the wilderness with you. It just turns out that this wasn't exactly one of the bravest things I've done."

"It was."

"It wasn't!"

"It was too."

"It . . . oh, listen to us, Jakkin. We sound like kids."

"I still think it was brave."

"Never mind. It's a silly argument anyway. Tell me what you found down there." She pointed to the center of the lake.

Excitedly he sketched out the underwater passage, the crystal cave, the river, the grassy slopes, and the reunion with the hatchlings.

"Then they're all right?" Akki asked, relief in her voice. "What about Tri-ssskkette's wing? All healed?"

"I . . . I didn't look," Jakkin admitted.

"Well, you *were* a bit busy," Akki conceded. "Besides, if she could fly all that way up the mountain, she must be doing fine. Wish we could heal as fast!"

"You can check it out when we get there," Jakkin said.

"I'll do that," Akki said a bit too brightly. "And now that I've practiced my underwater swimming—or at least my underwater nose holding—I'm ready to go. As long as you take my hand, Jakkin, I'll make it." Her voice had gotten high and brittle-sounding and she gave a little shiver, but she never stopped smiling.

Jakkin realized she wasn't feeling quite as brave as she was trying to appear, and he thought grimly that they'd both need Sssasha's heart for this.

"Why should I need Sssasha's heart?"

"Because . . . oh, never mind." Flustered, he could barely speak. She'd been able to pick up his thoughts, and he'd been so sure the automatic shielding worked. Perhaps it wasn't as complete as he hoped. Or maybe it worked just with dragons. Or self-involved dragons like Sssargon. Or perhaps it didn't work with someone who loved him, like Akki. Or . . . and then the further realization hit him. There was no more static in his mind.

"We've got to get out of here," he said.

"I'm ready." She started backing into the water.

"I mean back to the egg cave."

"The egg cave—don't be crazy. I can make it through the water, Jakkin. I *know* I can."

He put his hand out toward her. "I know you can, too, Akki. But we can't leave Auricle. They'll kill her. Just like the brown. Another bloody ceremony and more bones for the pile. We can't let them do it."

"Jakkin, we really don't have a choice. We have to save ourselves."

"No! We're not in danger. We can leave anytime. But we've got to save Auricle."

She turned away from him, shivering, and stared into the darkness. "We *are* in danger, Jakkin. In danger of becoming as brutish and dark-minded as these people. Can't you feel it? If we stay, sooner or later we'll be forced to join one of their bloody rituals, and then what will we be?"

"Akki, we're that already. Dragon breeders and stewards and trainers and all the rest of us on Austar, we've used and abused dragons for centuries. We've beaten them and eaten them, we've maimed and trained them as if they were simple animals. Even with all the evidence that they're more than that. And that's why we have to save the dragons, as many as we can—here and back at the nursery. At whatever the cost, Akki."

"Dragons? Plural? Do you have delusions of grandeur, Jakkin? Do you think you're a mighty hero? A moment ago you wanted to save only one dragon—Auricle."

"We have to save the hatchlings too."

"You can't save them all, Jakkin. There must be twenty or thirty dragons in here. And saving even one of them won't bring Heart's Blood back. Let's just go ourselves, before it's too late."

He ran his fingers through his hair and sighed. "You're not listening, Akki. I realize there's no such thing as a trade-off in guilt—these dragons for Heart's Blood. It's much more. I feel as if I'm seeing clearly for the first time. Why can't I make you see it too? Humans and dragons *together* for Austar's greater good."

"COME. COME. COME."

She stared at him, though her face had a strange listening look, as if one part of her was already caught in the web of

chanting. Then her thoughts came tumbling into his mind, obscuring the call for a moment. *"Together. Dragons and humans.
Oh, yes, Jakkin, yes. I understand."* Aloud, she added, "You really
don't need to save *all* the hatchlings here, only the females.
They set the males free when they're old enough to fend for
themselves. Didn't you know that? All the adult dragons in the
cave are female. When one comes into heat they stake her outside in the meadow and the wild males battle for possession.
That way the cave people don't have to worry about feeding and
caring for males, who are so unpredictable and difficult. The
males don't really matter to them anyway."

Jakkin snorted. "Don't matter?"

"No egg chamber," Akki said.

"Oh!"

"So you need me."

"Of course I need you," Jakkin said, pulling her into his arms.

She looked up into his face, her eyes suddenly clear and laughing. "Idiot—you need me because you still can't tell the difference between a male and a female hatchling—and I can. Some
dragon master you are."

He began to chuckle and she joined him, and their laughter
rose into a kind of hysteria until the chant began again, overwhelming them both. Then, like the rest of the cave people,
they marched unerringly through the tunnels toward the source
of the chant.

"COME. COME. COME."

22

They gathered on the edge of the meadow and watched the sun go down, a crowd of silent, staring people bound together by their thoughts.

Then, as if the setting sun released them to their tasks, the crowd surged forward into the great open space. Some of the men moved away from the rest, going toward a section of meadowland that was fallow and fuzzed over with new grass. A few women with hand tools headed toward the planted fields. The rest paused around the altar, which was splotched with dark shadows.

One woman began gathering up discarded robes, passing through the crowd to collect any that were left. She made piles of them on the stones, though Jakkin couldn't tell whether the piles had to do with size or with the amount of dirt or rips or tears in the robes. When he and Akki handed their wet robes to her, she glanced at them oddly, then placed them in a separate pile.

Makk threaded his way through the crowd, placing his hand

on an arm here, a shoulder there, choosing a cadre of workers, who in turn chose others. There were no arguments.

Coming toward him, Makk put his hand roughly on Jakkin's arm and his sending hurtled forward.

"Stay with others now. Pull cart."

Jakkin looked puzzled, and Makk pointed. When Jakkin made no immediate move Makk pushed him and hurled a sending after him.

"Go Brekk. Brekk knows."

Jakkin bowed his head at Makk, grateful the man hadn't noticed their absence. Searching out Akki, who'd been herded into a knot of women folding robes, he caught her eye and nodded. Then he concentrated on raising a heavy curtain over his thoughts with a tiny peephole showing through which he let out a carefully constructed sending. He was counting on the fact that these people, who shared every thought together, seemed to know nothing about acting or telling lies. His sending was a dark rendering of a dragon in pain. Not the pain of the slashed throat or the pain of a dragon in the Pit, but the pain of a hen whose birth canal was blocked. He drew on his memory of the days just past and flung the sending directly at Makk.

Makk's head jerked up. Looking around, he found Akki in the crowd and walked over to her swiftly, placing his hand on the back of her neck.

Jakkin forced himself to relax and lower the curtain, letting Makk's sending flood through him. He knew he'd be able to eavesdrop on it because he didn't subscribe to the code of privacy these people had fashioned for themselves.

Makk's sending was direct and clear. *"Go dragons. Heal."*

When Makk took his hand away, severing the intensity of the

connection, Jakkin insinuated a sending into Akki's still-open mind.

"*Good. Go to the dragons. Pretend Auricle's sick. Check her bonds. I'll be back as soon as I can.*" Then he closed his mind, turned, and sought out Brekk and the others, who had been detailed to the bone cart.

The journey seemed endless, even with ten men pulling and pushing the cart, for it was a heavy, unwieldy vehicle that could navigate the twisting passageways only with a great deal of human help. Pulling was worse than pushing, for they had to be strapped into leather harnesses. They stopped often and traded back and front groups.

Jakkin tried to keep track of the turnings so that he could make his escape. But he lost count of the numbered patches when someone fell against him, shoving him into the wall. He bumped his head so painfully, he forgot his careful tally.

It surprised him that they never came to the original lake where he'd tracked Auricle until he remembered that Akki had been taken on the other side of the lake and brought to the Place of Women by an entirely different route. So, he reasoned, his head still throbbing from the fall, there were many roads in this intricate mountain maze. That thought didn't comfort him.

He recognized only three of the men from the Ore shifts, one being one-eyed Brekk. If he'd had any hope that Brekk might treat him with an easy familiarity, he was wrong. As cart master, Brekk was a hard but fair leader and a tireless worker, taking many extra turns in the harness. In this he reminded Jakkin of Master Sarkkhan, who had outshoveled and outshouted every bonder at his nursery. Brekk's sendings were loud and snappish: "*Faster! Push! Here! Right turn! Stop!*"

In fact, they took only five rest stops altogether, and at each Brekk handed around several jugs filled with a cold, spicy red drink. Whether it was made of dragon's blood, like the hot protein drink takk, which was standard nursery fare, or of pressed berries, Jakkin couldn't tell. And he didn't ask. He drank it as eagerly as the rest of the men, for it was all they got on the long haul. When they'd each drunk their fill Brekk pushed them back to their feet with a powerful sending.

The cart and its bloody baggage rumbled on. Every once in a while one of the bones would tumble from the cart and someone would bend to retrieve it. Often the man picking up the bone would hold it up to his nose or lick it surreptitiously, snagging a piece of the stringy flesh. One time a *bande dominus* dropped down at Jakkin's feet, and when he stooped to pick it up he was aware that all the men were staring at him, waiting to see what he'd do. He stood up slowly and placed it reverently back on the cart, eyes smarting, for while it was in his hands he could feel— as if in a sending—the mental screams of the dying dragon. He walked away from the back of the cart into a side tunnel and was quietly sick.

The men ignored him completely after that, as if he'd failed some important test. Jakkin remembered, almost as if in a dream, the easy camaraderie of the bondhouse: the silly jokes, the noisy songs, the raucous, teasing laughter. Suddenly he missed all the bondboys and -girls he'd grown up with: the fat cook Kkarina, the sluggard Slakk, the hard-handed trainer Likkarn, even Errikkin, whose ingratiating ways had often irritated him. He thought of them with an exaggerated fondness even as he wondered what they'd make of Akki and him should they ever return.

When he had to get into the pull harness, Jakkin placed himself in the worst position, closest to the cart, where the wheels threatened at every pull to bang against his heels. But at that position the growling and creaking of the cart overwhelmed everything else and he could lose himself in his own thoughts, forgetting the sweat around him and the stale air of the cave.

By the time they reached the bone pile Jakkin was walking in his sleep, every muscle aching. After all, he'd been up long before the others and the underwater swim had taken its toll on his strength. Though he hadn't shared the frenzy of the night before, he'd also not shared all of the sleep. So he pulled with his eyes closed, following the lead of the straps, oblivious of the time. That's why it came as a surprise to him when they rolled to a stop in front of the great pile of whitened bones.

The other men dropped down where they stood, but Jakkin couldn't even move that much.

"*Sleep,*" Brekk sent. "*Work not-now.*"

Even before Jakkin could get his bearings, two of the men were snoring. When he finally got himself free of the harness, he found he couldn't just drop like the others into mindless sleep. He was too tired and too upset for that. So he stepped over the men in his way and walked up to the bone pile, craning his neck to look at the top. He remembered—how many days ago had it been?—when Akki and he had first seen the bones. They'd wondered what horrible beast could have done such a thing. And now they knew.

Walking slowly along the tunnel, he found his way back to the cave opening where he and Akki had first entered, pursued by the copter. He bent down and squinted at the bright light filtering through the interlacings of caught-ums. It was day again! They'd pulled the cart with its load of hollow bones the whole night long. It was clear that ordinary time had no meaning for these people. They went to hoe fields in the night. They slept when they dropped. All that mattered was metal—and blood. Dragon's blood. Because metal gave them their tools and blood gave them the ability to live in the cold, the ability to send, the ability to see the world through dragons' eyes.

And then a further thought hit him. *These* were the gifts— metal and the knowledge of the change through sheltering in the dragon's bloody birth chamber—that he and Akki had wanted to bring back to the daylit world.

He pushed aside the caught-ums, heedless of the briars that pierced his fingers. When he'd opened up a path he looked around. It would be so easy, he thought, to slip away down the hill, back to the three little caves where he and Akki had been so happy. But he couldn't slip away because there was Akki, left behind. And Auricle. And the hatchlings born of the slaughtered dragon. And because those three little caves were no longer an easy answer.

Finding a stick on the ground near the copse of spikka trees, he hefted it and went back through the thorny path, using the stick to unhook the caught-ums and close the way behind him. Then he found a place in the cave as far from the other sleepers as he dared, yet still within sight of them, curled his back against the wall, and slept.

23

They stacked the bones in an interlocking pattern and set them without ceremony next to the large pile. The unceremonious manner with which they treated the bones after the frenzied ritual of slaughter surprised Jakkin, and he was not asked to help. Because there were so many bones, it took a long time. When the men were done they began the long trip back without fussing. The cart was only marginally lighter on their return.

It occurred to Jakkin slowly, as they wound through the tunnels, that the pattern of bones was much too complex for these simple people to have invented. All their bowlware was new and simple; the carved statues and the ironwork had been created generations before by the original Makker and his friends. Over the years of inbreeding and silence the cave people's minds had grown dulled, lifeless. Jakkin knew enough about bloodlines to understand that. Dragon masters always said, *The wider the stock, the better the breed.*

The closer they got to the heart of the caves, Jakkin realized something else. He no longer feared the dark-minded Makk or the single-minded Brekk or any of the others. He pitied them.

But—he was quick to remind himself—that didn't mean they were any the less dangerous for it. After all, they'd killed a full-grown dragon with the crudest of weapons and their combined sendings could stun a man into a stupor. What he and Akki had were quick wits and an ability to communicate through words as well as sendings. He felt equal to any battle. But he would not let his confidence get in the way of caution.

When the men returned they ate in the Place of Women, for it was the largest cavern available. The ceremony being over, however, they ate apart from the women, though Jakkin noticed several couples signaling one another with their hands and then slipping away down the tunnels after the meal. Briefly he looked for Akki, thinking they might do the same. Then he remembered that he'd told Makk she was a healer, not to be treated like an ordinary woman. For her own safety, he had to keep her apart.

As he thought about Makk the man seemed to materialize beside him, a blunt sending coming through without the help of a touch.

"Go dragon. Help healer." The sending seemed grayed over, as if Makk were tired.

Jakkin nodded and, with Makk's initial help, found the right tunnel, which was marked with three lines of phosphorescence placed vertically, one horizontally. He took careful note of it. Then, hearing a sound behind him, he turned to see Brekk, his single eye glaring. Jakkin stopped and Brekk stopped. When he started forward again Brekk followed. So, Jakkin thought, he had been assigned a guard. And there was nothing secret about it. Something he or Akki had done must have made Makk wary. If he could only find out what, he'd act differently. After all, he didn't want to alert them ahead of time.

The tunnel opened into the egg room, bright with the light of many torches, and Jakkin saw Akki standing by a large stall behind a pale red dragon. Auricle had been moved into a layer's spot, though it would be months before she was ready to birth her clutch.

Auricle greeted Jakkin with a gray rainbow and arched her neck, but Akki's greeting was all in her face. Then her eyes shifted to Brekk, who had paused at the tunnel entrance to lean against the wall. Akki's eyebrows went up, and Jakkin, with his back to Brekk, formed a single silent word.

"Guard."

She nodded, turning back to the stall, and Jakkin followed her in. There were two women on their knees fussing over the dragon's nails and a third woman picking up straw and fewmets by hand and dropping them over the stall wall into a pushcart. By hand! Jakkin smiled wryly, wondering what his bondfriends, the lazy Slakk and the fastidious Errikkin, would say about that.

Sending carefully, he questioned Akki. *"How bad is this one?"* But he let the query broadcast to the women and Brekk.

"This one seems well, but when I examined her I found many potential problems. She needs exercise. And a bath." The picture she sent was of a greenish lake where a dragon frolicked and splashed.

"Careful," Jakkin whispered.

One of the women tending the nails looked up at the sound. Her mouth worked angrily, and her sending was sharp. *"Kkriah! Kkriah!"*

Brekk straightened up and started toward them, and Akki pushed out of the stall and met him halfway, putting her hand on his. *"The dragon must be moved. She must walk. Standing still so much makes the birth canal . . ."* Her sending faltered. She didn't find lying easy without words.

Jakkin broke in, finding the contact with Brekk made simpler by Akki's hand contact. *"Makes the birth canal close tight with sores. It is the way of this sickness."*

Akki took a deep breath, adding, *"How do I set her free?"*

Brekk shrugged off her hand and turned away from her, going back to the wall. His contempt shaped his sending. *"Woman's work."*

Wiping her filthy hands on her shirt, the woman who had been handling the fewmets signaled to Akki, *"Come. Come."* Her sending had more tone and rhythm than most.

Akki went back into the stall, Jakkin behind her. The woman bent down and opened the metal cuff with a quick flick of her hands. She held the cuff up. It had a simple snap-on lock.

Akki nodded, then turned away as if she were no longer interested in the mechanics of the bonds, sending instead to the women still tending Auricle's nails, *"Get water. Boil it. Very hot."*

They showed nothing in their faces but leaped up together and went out past Jakkin and Akki toward a far entryway.

"And you," Akki sent to the other woman, *"I need knives for the lancing. Boil them. And wash that filth from your hands."*

"Filth?" The sending was clearly puzzled.

"Go!" Akki let her exasperation show.

The woman left, wiping her hands down the front of her shirt.

Akki walked back to Brekk, who had been observing everything from his post, his single eye squinting. *"I need . . ."*

His sending cut across hers with the neat precision of a surgeon. *"I watch. I go no woman's way."*

Akki controlled her mouth and eyes with an effort, turned her back to him, and opened her mouth in a silent shout at Jakkin. "Help!"

Jakkin gave her a lopsided grin, bent, and quickly flicked open the other three chains and removed one from its setting in the wall. Then he signaled to Brekk. *"A man is needed here. The dragon must be led to water. Do not help the woman. Help me."* He never thought it would work.

But Brekk seemed relieved, and he came over at once to take hold of the dragon's ear, pulling it so roughly that Auricle backed out of the stall with jerky steps. Jakkin waited until the dragon obscured him, then he pulled Akki close and whispered in her ear, "We can go *now*. Get the hatchlings. I'll take care of him."

She moved quickly to the stall where the five hatchlings were sleeping, climbed over the fence, and disappeared. Jakkin, holding the chain behind him, walked up to Brekk, who still had Auricle's ear in a twisting hold.

Brekk may have heard his step, or a bit of Jakkin's anxiety may have leaked out around the edges of his mind barrier. At the last moment, just as Jakkin was bringing the heavy chain down upon his head, Brekk turned and raised his arm, taking most of the blow there, but the shock of it nevertheless tumbled him in front of the dragon's forefeet. She fell on her knees on top of his leg, and Jakkin heard the crack of bone. At the same moment a sending rocketed through him, full of pain and anger and astonishment. Then Brekk must have passed out because only a lingering shard of the sending remained in his head.

Jakkin grabbed for Auricle's ear. "Up!" he commanded aloud. His sending was more emphatic. The dragon slowly rose from her knees and Brekk, groaning out loud from the pain, turned his head aside.

Out of the corner of his eye Jakkin saw Akki climbing out of the stall, a single hatchling in her arms.

"Only one?"

"All the rest are males," she said.

"Are you sure?"

"Trust me."

"Then let's go." He pulled at her arm.

"I'd better do something about his leg," Akki said. "I don't know if they can set it. And—"

"We don't have time, Akki. And when he comes to, he's not going to be happy with us."

"Jakkin . . ."

He bent and picked up the chain and dangled it in front of her. "Trust me."

"Yes, sir!" she said, giving him a mock salute.

"Sometimes I wish you'd obey as fast as those other women!"

She whispered a curse that startled him because he hadn't known she knew such language. Then he grinned and gave her a hug. "But I'm satisfied," he added. "Trust me!" Throwing the chain down, he grabbed a fresh torch lying against the wall and lit it. "Now let's go!"

They trotted down the tunnel, careful to mask their thoughts, until Jakkin realized that the dragon's mind was wide open and broadcasting.

"Shut up," he commanded in a frantic sending, but either she didn't understand him or she just couldn't stop. And then the hatchling began to send a piping that bounced from wall to wall.

"Well, so much for a sneaky exit," he said. Akki's laughter bubbled through his mind, a laugh on the edge of hysteria. He had to concentrate hard to keep from responding to that hysteria himself.

Whether it was luck or memory that brought them to the lake Jakkin couldn't say, but within minutes they had found the pool with its green-white center. Akki set the hatchling down and stretched her arms.

"All right, Master Jakkin, now what?"

"We dive in." He pointed.

"You're the only one who can swim."

"I can pull you through and you can hold the hatchling. And Auricle *can* swim. I've seen her. And . . ."

Akki shook her head. "Gravid dragons have extra buoyancy."

"What's that?"

"It means she's going to float to the top."

"Why are you telling me this now?" Jakkin asked.

"Because you never gave me time before," Akki said. Then she looked down. "Besides, I just thought of it."

"Are you sure about the buoyancy?" Jakkin asked.

"Pretty sure," Akki said.

He sighed. "Well, I could run back and get those chains."

"What for?"

"Added weight."

"Not enough."

"Well, we have to try something." He scuffed his foot on the stones.

The dragon suddenly sent a gray-and-tan rainbow and there was that same plaintive tone: *"Man? Not-man?"*

That determined Jakkin. He sent her a command to lower her head, put his hands on each side of her face, below the earflaps, and stared deeply into her eyes. Speaking and sending at the same time, he said, "Auricle, thee must dive in the water and go under, fighting the buoyancy to get down to the light. Else the *men* will take you. They will take you and . . ." He summoned all his strength and showered her with the bloodiest sending he could manage. As he did so he felt Akki's hand on his back, lending her strength to his.

Startled, the dragon pulled back, nearly squashing the hatchling, who piped her distress. The piping stopped the dragon in her tracks. She turned and nuzzled the little one.

Akki pushed past Jakkin and put her hand on Auricle's broad flank. "They will kill this hatchling and those females in thy eggs as well." Her sending was even redder than the one Jakkin had managed, and it was filled with images of mothering and babies' blood and bonds.

Auricle lifted her head and a strange red light flickered in the dark shrouds of her eyes. It was the first time they had seen such a reaction from any of the cave dragons.

"Thou fighter," sent Jakkin. *"Thou beauty."*

Akki picked up the hatchling and they walked to the edge of the lake.

24

As they summoned the courage to dive, they heard the sound of footsteps in a nearby tunnel.

"Quick!" Jakkin's voice was suddenly hoarse. He plunged the torch into the water and, as it sizzled out, they were left in the half-shadows of the reflecting lake.

Akki waded in first, the hatchling clutched to her breast. Jakkin gave Auricle a shove with his shoulder against her flank, and she followed Akki into the shallows reluctantly. Jakkin entered the lake last, careful not to let his head get wet.

He whispered to Akki, "Comfort the little one but hold on tight. Once we go under she won't be getting any sendings from you and might panic. Take a deep breath when I tell you to and hold your nose."

Akki shifted the hatchling to her right arm and put her left hand up to her face in preparation.

"Good! Once we're under I'll grab the back of your shirt and tow you along. You won't have to do anything but hold on to the hatchling—and *don't breathe.*"

"I trust you," she whispered back.

He turned to the dragon. *"Open thine eyes underwater and swim toward the light. I cannot command thee under the water. Nor can any man."*

She answered him with a flash of color.

"Freedom awaits thee outside, my beauty. There are no blood rites there. Thee shall birth thy hatchlings and live to see them fly."

"?????"

"Jakkin," Akki hissed. "She doesn't know what you mean. Cave females never get to fly."

"Well, they've seen the wild males flying, haven't they?" He sent Auricle a picture of a male dragon in the sky circling a female below. *"That is flying, my beauty."*

"!!!!!"

The running footsteps got nearer, honing in on the sendings, and the first tentative feelers from the searchers drifted into their minds.

"Take a deep breath, Akki. Now!" Jakkin said. "Dive!"

The dragon went first, her tail whacking the water with a sound as loud as a thunderbolt, drenching them in the process. Akki was next, taking a noisy breath and ducking under. Jakkin followed immediately, grabbing a handful of her shirt back. With a powerful kick, he began to tow her down toward the inviting green-and-gold light.

As he swam Jakkin felt as if he were moving slowly through a nightmare. Each stroke seemed to take forever. Glancing back, all he could see of Akki was a dark, amorphous figure. He hoped she was still holding the hatchling because he couldn't tell. Her dead weight slowed his progress. By the time they'd come to the light-colored water, he was practically out of breath and he knew there was still a long passage under rock before he could start toward the surface again.

Ahead of him the green-gold light suddenly went dark and he felt the cold water chill his bones. For a second he considered surrendering himself to the cold. All he needed was one quick intake of breath and the aching in his chest and lungs would be gone forever. Then he thought about Sssasha and Sssargon and Heart's Blood. They flashed across his thoughts like pictures on a screen. At that very moment the light returned full force and he saw the outline of a tail moving ahead of him. Auricle's enormous body had been blocking the light. He'd known it subconsciously and that was why he'd thought about the other dragons. Relieved, he kicked his feet extra hard and surged forward, ignoring the fact that he'd no breath left, that he couldn't feel his towing arm, that his ears were popping. He kept swimming because it was the only thing he *could* do, for Akki and the hatchling and himself.

And then he was past the rocky overhang and into the pulsing light, bursting up into the air, sobbing and gasping at the same time. Already on the rock ledge, Auricle was shaking herself all over, spraying the cave with water and rainbows.

Jakkin swam toward the ledge, found a footing in the shallower water, and hauled Akki behind him. Her eyes were still squeezed shut, her left hand cupped over her nose. He grabbed the hand and pulled it away, and for a moment she fought him.

"It's all right, Akki," he cried, his voice ragged. "We've made it. We're here."

She opened her eyes slowly, all the while taking in great gulps of air. Her eyelids fluttered and her pupils seemed filmed over and unfocused. The hatchling began to squirm in her arm. They both moved with a slow deliberation, as if they were still under-water.

"Jakkin," she whispered. Then louder: "Jakkin?" Opening her right arm as if it hurt to do so, she dropped the hatchling into the water. It paddled in awkward circles until Auricle stuck her long neck out and nosed the dragonling to the ledge. It scrambled up, leaving patches of eggskin on the rocks.

Jakkin and Akki lay side by side in the shallows for a minute, neither one with enough energy to move or speak further. Their breathing was rapid and Jakkin could feel the pounding of his heart. After a while he tried flexing his hand, the one that had held on to Akki's shirt. His fingers were cramped and his thumb ached.

"You're no lightweight," he said at last. "Even in the water."

Stretching her right arm, Akki smiled but kept her eyes closed. "Neither was the hatchling. I don't think my arm will ever be the same."

Behind them, on the ledge, the hatchling piped for attention until Auricle stopped its noise with a lick of her tongue, simultaneously removing another small patch of eggskin.

"How do we get out of here?" Akki asked, sitting up at last. "There's only one tunnel and it's full of water."

"We float through," Jakkin said. Noticing Akki's dismayed face, he added, "We don't have to go under again. The river does all the work. Trust me. We just lie on our backs and it takes us through. I promise I'll hold on to you."

Akki nodded, but they had to wait a few minutes more, until their minds were free of the static and Jakkin could give Auricle her instructions. Then the dragon waddled into the water, where Jakkin placed the hatchling on her broad back, close up to the neck.

"Stay there," he warned the hatchling with a stern sending, and touched it on the nose. *"There thee will be safe, little one."*

The hatchling piped an answer, but whether it understood, Jakkin wasn't sure. It looked as if it did, cocking its head to one side, a patch of eggskin peeling from its nose.

"The river is slow," he sent to Auricle. *"There is nothing to fear."* He looked again at the hatchling and wondered if it was afraid. Communication with it would be uncertain for days, even weeks. After all, it was only a baby.

"It's a she, remember?" Akki's voice had recovered much of its lighthearted quality.

"You stay out of my mind!" Jakkin said gruffly. "Unless I invite you in. That's one thing the cave people have right."

"The *only* thing," Akki added.

"Concentrate on floating," Jakkin said. "The rest is easy."

The current had already caught the dragon and was moving her along in a slow, majestic fashion. Jakkin was reminded of the way Sssasha had floated in the sky. He took Akki's hand and they pushed off into the middle of the lake. Soon they, too, were caught by the river's pull.

"The hard part is over," he called. "Relax and enjoy this."

Akki, her body stiff, shouted back, "Why do I wish you hadn't said that?"

"Everything's going to be just fine," Jakkin shouted. "Trust me!"

They floated through the round tunnel opening to the outside, where the sun was just rising on a new Austarian day.

25

As they floated they watched the sky, blue and unmarred by clouds. First one black dot, then a second, then three more suddenly peppered the horizon, rising and coming together in a triangular formation that moved closer and closer.

"Look!" Jakkin shouted, waving his free hand in the air. A wave swamped them, causing him to lose his grip on Akki's hand. They both went under, and Jakkin swam desperately after her, taking nearly a dozen strokes before he caught up with her again.

Grabbing a handful of her shirt, he headed them both toward the riverbank. Once his feet touched bottom he stood up, surrendering himself to a coughing fit. Akki found her footing at the same time and began pounding him on the back. Then they scrambled up the grassy slope and stared up at the sky.

The five dots had become much larger, resolving themselves into dragon shapes. Jakkin knew they had to be Heart's Blood's hatchlings, but he couldn't reach their minds because his now crackled with static from his recent ducking in the water. He waved frantically instead.

But the dragons weren't watching him. They were hovering over a place farther downriver. It was Akki who understood first.

"Auricle!" she cried. "It's Auricle they're watching. She's still in the water."

Jakkin shaded his eyes, following the path of the twisting river until he could just make out Auricle's lumpish form. Knowing he couldn't reach her with a sending until the static cleared, he shouted, "Get out! Auricle—get out now!" But his voice couldn't compete with the sound of the water.

Akki grabbed his arm. "What's that sound, Jakkin?"

"You mean the crackle? The static? Or the river?"

"No, there's another sound. A kind of growling."

"I don't know. I heard it before. Why?"

They both strained to listen for a moment, and then Akki said softly, "Waterfall!"

Without another word they began to race along the grassy border, screaming as they went, even though they knew it was futile. Auricle couldn't hear them. At last they gave up screaming because the more they yelled, the less breath they had for running.

For a while they seemed to be gaining on the waterborne dragon, for her progress was slowed by the many broad river bends. Several times she was spun around completely, bouncing off dangerous-looking rocks. They could see the hatchling balanced on her back. And once she wallowed for a moment in a patch of reeds close to the far shore, giving them time to close the gap. But then the current caught her again and carried her farther downstream. As she approached the place where the river and land dropped away precipitously into the waterfall, things seemed to speed up and she was buffeted from side to side by the ever-increasing white waves, further endangering the hatchling clinging to her back.

Just then Jakkin's mind cleared and he stopped in order to read the frantic colors of Sssargon's sending. Akki began to slow down as well, and he waved her past.

"*Sssargon worries. Sssargon calls. Sssargon hears nothing.*"

More sensibly, Sssasha broadcast advice to the drifting dragon: "*Paddle thy wings. Use thy feet. Come to the shore.*"

But it was soon apparent to all of them that Auricle was too frightened to do anything but let the current carry her on. Her mind was filled with the same dull terror that Jakkin had first heard in the caves. He guessed the fighter's light in her eyes would be gone.

He sent instructions to the larger hatchlings. "*Go in the water with her. Push her to the shore. Triplets—be my eyes and ears. Stay above. Let me see all.*"

Without waiting for an answer he began to run again, concentrating on the precarious footing, for the grass was slippery near the river.

Sssargon launched himself into the water, further drenching Auricle. One of his wings buffeted her and she spun around helplessly. Then Sssasha dropped into the river on Auricle's other side. Keeping her between them, they tried to ease her to the shore, but by now the water was churning angrily and a wild froth filled the air. All three were perilously close to the edge of the falls.

Standing on the bank, Akki urged them out with frantic shouts and sendings, but Sssargon's running commentaries had ceased and so had Sssasha's calm murmurings. Either they were all too intent on staying afloat or the water had once again performed its own strange silencing.

Jakkin caught up with Akki, shouting to her above the noise of the river, "It's no good trying to send, Akki. They must have each gone under at least once. The water's cut off any sendings. I don't understand it. The water in the oasis where I trained Heart's Blood never did this."

"Minerals, Jakkin. The same minerals that the cavefolk mined. That has to be it. It has to be. It has—"

He grabbed her arm, wanting to shake her into silence, and at the touch was drawn into the maelstrom of her mind. Taking a deep breath, he forced himself to blanket them both with a calming blue. Akki finally stopped mind-babbling.

In the water the three dragons were now fighting the tossing current individually, spinning away from one another, lost in separate whirlpools.

"Why don't Sssasha and Sssargon get out?" Jakkin cried.

"Because, you idiot, you told them to save her. And they'll do whatever you ask. You're both father and mother to them. They'll die rather than disappoint . . ." She closed her mouth but her mind finished off the thought and Jakkin felt both hot and cold at its touch.

And then the river took the three dragons and tipped them over the edge of the world.

Rushing to the cliffside, Jakkin cast a sending up. *"Tri-sss, be my eyes."*

Immediately a picture formed in his mind: three large figures tumbling down the falls. Sssargon, the heaviest, was first. For a moment he stopped, caught on a rocky outcropping. Then he pushed straight out from the water, plummeting through the air, his wet wings too heavy to carry him. As the wind dried his scaly feathers he unfurled his wings with a loud crack. Pumping them once, he flew straight back toward the falls.

"No!" Jakkin shouted.

Deaf to both sound and sending, Sssargon made one or two feints at the falls and then found Sssasha. He plucked her out of the vertical water and dropped her free.

Overweighed by the water she, too, fell straight down. Then suddenly she flipped, shot her wings out, and backwinged away from the plunging water.

"What about Auricle?" shouted Akki.

As if sensing the question, Sssargon and Sssasha both turned back to the falls. Jakkin could see through Tri-sss' eyes that Auricle was no longer falling but clinging to a rocky outjut, though water was steadily pounding around her. There was no sign of the hatchling.

As if on a signal, Sssargon and Sssasha dashed into the falls at the same moment, emerging again with the drenched Auricle in their claws. Once free of the water, they dropped her. She fell like a stone, tumbling end over end in the glistening air.

"She doesn't know how to fly," screamed Akki. "She's . . ."

Even though they couldn't hear her, Sssasha and Sssargon had come to the same conclusion. Sssargon swept his wings back hard against his sides and followed Auricle in a long, perilous stoop, diving headfirst toward the ground. Passing Auricle, he flipped over, snapped his wings open once he was below her, and readied himself to cushion her fall.

"If she hits him . . ." Akki began.

"She'll kill them both," Jakkin said, his voice flat. He closed his eyes, but Tri-sss's unrelenting sendings denied him any relief.

Just fifty feet from the ground, as if the air itself had ripped them open, Auricle's wings spread, fluttered, and caught an updraft that sent her into an off-balance soar.

Surprised, Sssargon almost fell to the ground anyway. At the last moment he turned and pumped his wings, scraping one on a large rock. Then he sailed up to Auricle's right. Sssasha banked and flew down to her left, sending a bemused thought into Jakkin's mind:

"No splat!"

"No splat indeed," Jakkin whispered. He threw his arms around Akki, unashamed of the tears running down his cheeks.

A horrible thought hit them both at the same time, though it was Akki who said it aloud.

"The hatchling!"

Already aware of the danger, the triplets were broadcasting simultaneous signals of distress: flashes of haunch and head as the little dragon tumbled head over heels through the water all the way down the treacherous falls.

It took Jakkin and Akki nearly an hour to scramble down the cliffside, but when they got to the bottom, where the falls puddled into several rocky pools before fanning out into five small fingerlike rivers, there were the triplets and Sssasha, Sssargon, and Auricle, all standing over the dragonling.

Akki screamed, "You didn't tell us! You let us think she was dead." She ran over and grabbed up the hatchling, who wriggled delightedly in her arms.

A splash of chuckles ran through Jakkin's head. *"No splat, no splat, no splat."*

Akki turned to him, her eyes full of laughter. "Jakkin, don't you see—proof positive that they're not just animals. Animals couldn't play a practical joke." She nuzzled the hatchling.

Jakkin nodded. "But what really happened?" he asked, letting his mind send the question to them.

It took many minutes of patchworked sendings before he and

Akki really understood the whole thing. Each dragon added a part or contradicted another. But finally the story came clear. The hatchling, being so small, had tumbled easily and landed in the pooling water at the bottom of the falls without hitting any rocks along the way. She was hardly the worse for her hazardous trip and, in fact, had rather enjoyed it all.

If dragons could smile, they smiled.

Without her medkit Akki couldn't do much for the scratches and bruises. Sssasha had torn her secundum while carrying Auricle, and the endpiece of Sssargon's left wing was ripped. Auricle was missing some scales in both wings and there was blood on her nose. None of it was serious. Only the hatchling seemed unbruised, though its eggskin was peeling off more quickly than was natural.

"We'll have to be careful with her," Akki cautioned, "or she'll get sunburned on her new scales."

The dragons licked their wounds and Akki reminded Jakkin that that was, after all, the best medicine for them, since there was something in the saliva that promoted healing.

"What really worries me, though," Akki said later, gesturing to Auricle, "are her eggs. She's taken quite a beating these last few hours. It may not show on the outside but . . ." She let the sentence dangle.

"Even if she loses this clutch," Jakkin said, "it won't be so bad. She'll be able to have another. And at least she's alive."

"Alive—and lost. Just like the rest of us," Akki said.

Sssasha, who'd been listening in on their thoughts, intruded a sending.

"What pain?"

"No pain," Jakkin sent back.

"*Yes, pain,*" Sssasha said, coming over to stick her nose against Jakkin's chest.

"*We're lost, Sssasha,*" Akki sent.

"*Not lost. Trust me.*"

Jakkin looked at Akki and they burst out laughing at the same time. Sssasha joined in with tiny, popping, rainbow-colored bubbles that seemed to march across a vast sandy plain.

26

Exhausted, they slept away the rest of the morning in a tight circle of dragons and humans. Akki woke before Jakkin, then shook him furiously.

"Sssasha and Sssargon are gone," she said.

Jakkin opened an eye, for a moment stunned by the sun's glare. He yawned and stretched, surprised at how stiff his body was, and remembered only slowly why his left hand was cramped and aching.

"Jakkin, wake up. Sssasha and Sssargon are gone."

"They're probably just off grazing, Akki." He rubbed his left hand slowly.

"There's enough grazing right here," Akki said, her sweeping hand taking in all the land around the fingerlike rivulets.

Jakkin nodded. The grass was rich and thick, and in the drier places burnwort and blisterweed were both growing in abundance, the red stalks a sign of healthy plants. Smoke ghosts swirled over the patches of wort and weed, signaling they were almost ready to leaf out.

"And I can't hear them," Akki said.

"You're worrying too much, Akki."

"I can't hear them, but I do hear something else," she said. "Listen!"

Shrugging, he listened. He could hear the *pop-pop* of the dragons' breath as Auricle and the triplets slept easily. He could hear the dull roar of the falls and beyond that a kind of echo that might have been the river. Nearer were the *swish-swash* sounds of the five streams lazing between banks. He could hear the *pee-up-up* of some river-edge creature protesting their presence, and the constant chittering of insects.

"I'm listening," he said as his mind filled with dragon dreams: soft, unfocused points of pulsing light, with darker undertones he suspected belonged to Auricle.

"Then you hear it?"

Shaking his head, Jakkin was puzzled. He tried to listen harder. And then he heard a strange faraway *chuffing*, deeper than the dragon snores but higher than the roar of the falls. He knew that sound.

"Copter!" he said, jumping up.

Akki grabbed his arm. "What will we do? Where can we hide?"

They'd been sleeping near the smallest of the five rivulets, for the grass was soft and sweet and relatively dry. But there were no rocks or trees to hide behind, and the falls were too far away.

"We could hide under the dragons," Akki said. "If they were on their feet, we could lie down under Auricle and the others could crowd around." She ran over to the dragons and started pulling on their earflaps to rouse them.

The copter sounds came closer even as the sleeping dragons began to wake. Auricle lumbered to her feet, sending a jumbled message, gray and questioning, but the triplets, still stretched out on the ground, sent a different thought:

"Man coming. Man coming. Man coming."

"Akki," Jakkin said sharply.

She turned at his tone and looked up at him.

"Akki—no." This time his voice was soft, almost pleading. "No more hiding. No more running. It's time to face this . . . this *man coming.* Face him and go home." He hadn't known what he was going to say until the words came tumbling out of his mouth, and then he realized he'd known it all along. The escape from the mountain hadn't been a running-away-*from.* It had been a running-away-*to.*

"Think, Jakkin, think." Her mind sent him arrowpoints of orange and red, charged with electricity. "We don't know who's in that copter, enemy or friend."

"It could be a stranger," Jakkin said. "Someone just out for a flight. One chance in three."

"Remember what you said when we first ran off from the copter, Jakkin. That whoever is in the copter *has* to be looking for us." She began to braid the ends of her hair nervously.

He walked over to her and put his arms around her, drinking in the clean grass and river smell in her hair. "Akki, listen to me. With your ears and heart and mind this time." He sent her a picture of a damned-up river, then slowly opened the floodgates. A wall of green water tumbled through, threatening to overwhelm her.

"It's time for us to open those gates, Akki."

"I don't know what you mean."

"Time to grow up and time to help Austar grow up too."

She pulled away from him and stared at the ground. "Will you be telling them about the egg chamber and how it changes a person, how it lets us live in the cold and see the world through dragons' ears and eyes? If you do, you know, you'll be condemning every female dragon on Austar to an early death."

He shook his head.

"And will you tell them about the metal to be had inside these mountains? Because if they find that metal, they find the cave people. And then they'll find the secret of the change. Goodbye, dragons."

"*Them,* Akki? Who do you mean?"

"The rebels or the wardens—the bad guys. The ones who've been after us."

"Don't just worry about the rebels and the wardens, Akki," Jakkin said. "If it's a matter of metal and the change, *everyone* will be a bad guy. Even the good ones like Dr. Henkky and Golden and Likkarn. For all the *right* reasons, they'll slaughter the dragons."

"Then what will you tell them? All of them?"

Jakkin shook his head. "Very little at first."

She bit her lip. "Listen, Jakkin, I'm a doctor. Or at least I'm almost one. I bet I could help find some *other* way, other than killing dragons, to give everyone what they want—dragons' ears and eyes."

He nodded.

"But if we can't say anything, how are we going to help Austar grow up?"

He pulled her toward him again. "Slowly," he said. "From the nursery on. That's how babies grow."

"It won't be easy."

"Growing up never is," he said. "I guess I'm just understanding that."

She kissed him, her hands cool on either side of his face. And the flooding river of his sending turned a blue-green and then they needed no more words.

They were still in each other's arms when the copter came into view around the mountainside. Flanking it were Sssargon and Sssasha, though well out of range of the twirling blades.

Slowly the copter settled between two of the streams. The dragons hovered until the rotors stopped whirling, then they made perfect, graceful landings.

"Show-offs!" Akki whispered, but her arm tensed about Jakkin's waist.

The copter door opened and a man in a Federation uniform got out. He was a slim man who walked with a movement that was both calculating and loose. As he got closer Jakkin could see the blue of his eyes under beetling brows.

"Hello, Akki. Hello, Jakkin," he said, his voice full of warmth.

"Golden! It's Golden," Akki cried, letting go of Jakkin and running over to the man. "We thought you were dead."

Golden smiled and the scar on his cheek bunched. Jakkin was sure that this time it was a real scar, not the fake one he'd used so often in the past.

"The same was said about the two of you—in certain quarters. But the reports of our deaths, as an old Earth writer once said of himself, have obviously been grossly exaggerated." He disentangled himself from Akki's arms. "Be careful with me, Akki. These bones don't knit as swiftly as your young ones. Henkky hasn't been too pleased with my progress these last months. I seem to have several painful reminders of our last—outing—together."

They all laughed and Akki touched the scar on his cheek.

Jakkin shook his hand, surprised at the strength in the grip, and said, "You don't seem surprised to see us."

"I am—and I'm not," Golden said. "Can you say the same?"

"We're definitely surprised," admitted Jakkin.

"We thought you'd be wardens or rebels," Akki said.

Golden looked at them thoughtfully. "But still you didn't try to run off." He paused. "I'd say you've done a lot of thinking—"

"And growing up," Akki said.

"I always thought you two were remarkably grown-up for your age," Golden said. "Or I wouldn't have involved you in spying and—"

"Why are you here?" asked Jakkin. "Why now?"

"To find you, obviously. And bring you back."

Akki smiled but Jakkin's eyes narrowed. "Bring us back how? As friends? As prisoners? As criminals? As runaways?"

"Not exactly prisoners, otherwise I'd be home and the wardens would be here. But not exactly free either. Let's say you are wards of the state."

At their puzzled glances, he added, "An offworld term I learned long ago. You see, I ran the investigation from my hospital bed—when Henkky allowed me!—and cleared you two of the charges of planting the bomb at Rokk Major."

"How many people were hurt?" Akki asked.

"And how many dragons?" Jakkin added.

"Enough," Golden said.

"How many?" Jakkin insisted.

"Thirty-seven were killed outright," Golden said.

"And Sarkkhan?" Jakkin asked.

"And Sarkkhan," Golden said, nodding.

A small sigh escaped Akki's lips but nothing more. It was an old wound, and she'd never really believed her father had a chance of escaping. But Jakkin put his hand on her arm and her eyes widened.

"Hundreds of others were injured, some very seriously. At least twenty more died of their wounds over the next few months."

"And the dragons?" Jakkin asked again.

"Forty maimed."

"And sent to the Stews," Akki whispered.

Golden nodded. "It was the worst disaster Austar has ever known. The Federation sent men and supplies, but the price was high. They wanted to run the search for you themselves and it took a lot of arguing in the Senate to rule that out. Meanwhile, Captain Kkalkkav and his wardens declared you dead. He wasn't pleased when I proved your innocence from my hospital bed. It took away his hero status and made him little better than a murderer. He forgot how well connected I am. But he forgave me when I found him Akki's old cell of rebels and he and his men broke it—except for the leader."

"Number One!" Akki breathed.

"Your Number One got away. His name, by the way, is Swarts."

"There's no double *K* in that name," said Jakkin. "Is he a master?"

"Oh, yes," Golden said.

"Then why is he a rebel? I thought only KKs were involved in trying to bring down the system." Jakkin looked puzzled.

Golden smiled. "Still the innocent, Jakkin? There are as many masters who hate the bond system as bonders."

Akki whispered, "Golden is a master, Jakkin."

Golden ignored her and continued, "Wanting freedom to run a world is not a dream limited to the underclasses. Every master is not rich. Every bonder is not poor. And every rebel is not fighting to set his *brother* free, Jakkin. There are as many reasons as rebels."

Jakkin looked down at the ground, chafing under Golden's lecture.

"But freedom *is* a good and noble goal, Jakkin. I managed to get some of the best of the rebel ideas cleaned up and passed into law from my hospital bed. We set the bonders free. That brought a good many rebels into our camp, I'll tell you. Except for the ones like Swarts, whose interest is more domination than nation. You'd be surprised how effective and popular a man can become when he's lying near death and issuing pleas through an attractive lady doctor!"

"I don't understand," Akki said. "If you've cleared us of the Pit bombing and all bonders are free, why aren't we—*exactly?*"

"Because, my dear Akki," said Golden, putting his hands on her shoulders, "I cleared the names of a romantic young *dead* couple. Once you return alive—well, there are bound to be some difficult questions, which, as my wards and prisoners, you won't be obliged to answer."

"What kind of questions?" asked Jakkin, sure he already knew.

"Questions such as why you haven't frozen to death many times over during Dark After? How did you escape the night you were left? Where have you been living all this time? Which, by the way, no one will know because I destroyed the pots and garlands in your caves."

"You found the caves?" Akki asked, her voice rough. "You destroyed everything?"

"Everything," Golden said. "I hated to do it. It was clear you'd worked hard to make those caves your home."

"One of them was even named after you," said Akki in a small voice.

"How did you find them?" Jakkin asked.

Golden shrugged. "Bones," he said. "The tattletale of bones. We found Heart's Blood's bones—but we didn't find yours."

"*We?*" Jakkin and Akki asked together.

"Don't worry. *We* wasn't Kkalkkav or any of his minions. He really hasn't the brains to assume you were anything but dead. It was Likkarn."

"Likkarn!" Jakkin exclaimed.

"Funny old man. Years ago he'd managed to live for a while in the foothills, holed up with dragons in a cave. He knew it *could* be done, just didn't know if it had been done by the two of you. What he said was 'Jakkin and Akki have the luck and lust for it,' meaning if it could be done, you two could do it. He also said that if you hadn't made it, then we should bring back your bones and bury them at home. *'Among friends.'* That's what he said. He told me that in the hospital. We had a long time there together and I found him a fascinating, complicated man."

"He was in the hospital too?"

"He'd had both arms and a leg broken when he fought off the wardens at the nursery to buy us running time, remember?" Golden said. "And he lost the use of one eye as well. Old bones heal slowly. But he says he's the better for it, for he'd been off the weed all that time. And I don't think he's going to backslide, either."

"So you went up to the caves together?" Akki said. "That must have been difficult for him."

"We took a copter and set it down in the meadow where your red was killed. I could hardly bring myself to look at the bones. Likkarn did that. He looked—and laughed out loud. Brought me right over. 'I told you they got luck and lust,' he said. There wasn't a human bone among them. Well, you'd know that, of course.

"We went along the pathway on three different days, checking the caves. Found three places with your stamp on them. We tore apart the mattresses and garlands, threw the pots over the cliffside."

"Oh," Akki said.

"But how'd you know to find us *here?*" asked Jakkin.

Golden gestured with his head toward the dragons. "They told us. The big ones."

Sssargon and Sssasha, squatting on their haunches on either side of the copter, managed to look bored.

"They'd been coming and going almost daily at the nursery these last two weeks, circling and then landing by the incubarn. Likkarn thought he recognized them as Heart's Blood's hatchlings. Said that golden slash on the nose of that one was a dead giveaway."

Jakkin sent a quick burst of color toward Sssasha, which she returned with a rainbow.

"Likkarn seemed to manage some kind of connection with them," Golden continued. "Even claimed he could understand them. I said he was a good guesser."

"Very good guesser," Akki said, laughing.

Golden rubbed his nose with his forefinger. "Of course, maybe there's more to it than I know." He said it carefully.

Akki looked at Jakkin, her eyes widening.

"Maybe," said Jakkin. "And maybe not. As your wards we won't be answering questions, or so you said."

"That's right," Golden answered. "That's what I said."

"Then what comes next?" Jakkin asked.

"I'll take you back to the nursery farm now," said Golden. "If you're ready to come."

"We're ready," Jakkin said.

Akki nodded her agreement and reached down to pick up the hatchling, who had been lying against her ankles. The hatchling snuggled into her arms, its tail looped around her wrist.

Jakkin watched Golden and Akki climb into the copter. He walked over to Auricle and placed his hands on either side of her broad head.

"Thou beauty," he sent. *"Try thy wings once more and, if thee will, follow the others to the place where we live, the nursery. It will be a safe place for thee and thy eggs."*

He didn't wait for an answer. Whether she came to the farm or stayed in the world, she was free of the tyranny of the caves. That was all that mattered now.

Climbing into the copter, Jakkin sat behind Akki in a seat that seemed much too soft for comfort. Golden turned and showed him how to buckle his seat belt across his lap. Then he turned back to the copter console. As the great machine engine started up the noise was deafening.

Golden shouted, his voice barely rising above the churring of the rotors, "We won't be able to talk much until we're down again. Too loud." He pointed to the ceiling, then bent to fiddle with the controls, a panel of winking, blinking lights that reminded Jakkin of fighting dragons' eyes.

Jakkin put his hand on Akki's shoulder and their minds touched, a clear, clean, silent meeting. Then he looked out the window as the copter rose into the air. Austar stretched out below him in great swatches of color. He could see the dark mountain with its sharp, jagged peaks and the massive gray cliff-faces pocked with caves. He could see tan patches of desert where five ribbons of blue water fanned out from the darker blue of a pool, and the white froth of the waterfall. Running into the waterfall was a blue-black river that gushed from the mountainside like blood from a wound.

He sent a message to Akki full of wonder and light. *"This . . . this is true dragon sight, Akki. We're like dragons in flight above our world."*

Mind-to-mind they talked of it all the way back to the nursery and home.

WHITE RIVER LIBRARY
Franklin-Johnson County System
Franklin, IN 46131

About the Author

Jane Yolen is well known for her more than eighty books for children and young adults and for her activities as a teacher and lecturer. Both *Dragon's Blood* and *Heart's Blood*, the first two books of the Pit Dragon trilogy, were chosen as American Library Association Best Books.

A native of New York City, Jane Yolen grew up in Westport, Connecticut, and was graduated from Smith College, where she taught for a number of years. She is the president of the Science Fiction Writers of America as well as on the Board of Directors for the Society of Children's Book Writers. With her husband and three grown children, she lives in the small New England town of Hatfield, Massachusetts.